Rogue's Gold

"Rogue's Gold"

W. W. Lee

Walker and Company
New York

First published in the United States of America in 1989
by Walker Publishing Company, Inc.

Published simultaneously in Canada by Thomas Allen & Son
Canada, Limited, Markham, Ontario.

Library of Congress Cataloging-in-Publication Data

Lee, W. W. (Wendi W.)
Rogue's gold.
I. Title.
PS3562.E3663R64   1989   813'.54   89-5770
ISBN 0-8027-4096-0
JIMØ39Ø2
Printed in the United States of America

10 9 8 7 6 5 4 3 2 1

For my grandmother, Mabel Carlson
With love

ACKNOWLEDGMENTS

THIS book could not have been written without the support and generous contributions of the following—thanks to them all: Max Collins and Paul Thomas for their invaluable assistance, above and beyond the call of duty or friendship, in the preparation of the manuscript; my agent, Barb Peekner—and Ed Gorman for introducing me to her; my editor, Jackie Johnson, for her insightful suggestions along the way; Gerard Jones and Tom DeFalco for their words of encouragement; and last but not least, Terry.

Rogue's Gold

CHAPTER 1

ELIJAH Stearns scratched at his six-day growth of salt-and-pepper whiskers as he rode his horse past the Grant's Pass jailhouse. He caught sight of the young redheaded deputy, Jim Carver, sitting outside the marshal's office. Elijah called to him, "Morning, Jim. Nice day."

The deputy looked up from cleaning his gun, his pockmarked face blank with concentration, then nodded to Elijah. "Sure is. You look like you're going somewhere, Lije."

"Heading to Jacksonville for a spell." Noticing a big stocky man stepping out of the jailhouse door, Lije greeted him, too. "How's the gout this morning, Marshal?"

Henry Stubbs, a wad of tobacco in his cheek, absently rubbed his elbow. "Not as bad as when it rains, Lije." He looked with mild surprise at Lije's packed horse. "You taking some gold to Jacksonville today?"

Lije looked around the nearly empty streets uneasily. He saw a fellow miner named Dewey enter a dry goods store.

"Aw, now, Marshal," Lije said. "Why don't you go and tell the whole town about it? I want to leave quietly so's no one knows."

Carver looked up sharply, shrugged, and went back to checking the chambers of his gun. The marshal seemed amused. "Why, Lije. What kind of lawman do

1

you think I am? No one's here but you, me, and the deputy. Even if Dewey saw you, he was too far away to hear what I said. Besides, you know he's a trustworthy fellow. This here's a respectable town now."

Lije knew that Stubbs was proud of his reputation. With all the gold miners and the nearby logging camp, Grant's Pass could be an easy mark for outlaws lured to town by the regular monthly wages paid to the loggers and the occasional boon from a gold mine. But Marshal Stubbs had cleaned up the town, making it safe for those with dust and money to spend it at the saloons and general stores here.

Of course, "road withdrawals" did happen, but the robberies were confined to the road that led from Grant's Pass to Jacksonville. The last logging camp payroll scheduled to come through never made it. Just five miles from town, the stage was ambushed. Stubbs had rounded up a posse and searched the area without luck, concluding that the bandits were already crossing the mountains to Klamath Falls or backtracking to some small way station such as Ashland.

And now Elijah Stearns was taking his gold to the bank in Jacksonville. He mined up in the hills near the Rogue River and a few days ago, after working his claim for four years, he had struck a vein every miner dreamed about. But few ever struck a lode as rich as this one, and Lije was not about to take his luck for granted as he made his way to Jacksonville.

"I expect," Stubbs said, "you heard about them road withdrawals, Lije."

Lije was checking his saddle for loose fittings. He turned to Stubbs. "Reckon now's as good a time to go as any. Guess I'll have to take my chances."

"What if you get robbed? You worked long and hard

for that gold." Stubbs worked the tobacco juice around in his mouth before aiming the spit off to his right. "Ain't right for some road agents to make off with your dust."

Lije paused briefly to consider Stubbs's flawless logic. "Gotta go now. The next load'll be heavier and I won't be able to haul it all in at once. Too bad there isn't a bank here in town." Lije pulled out his Colt and loaded the chambers. "But don't worry, Marshal. Those bandits will be taking a chance, too. I'm packing a couple of rifles and my Colt. If it comes to that, one of these shooters will hit a target." Lije pulled a yellow bandanna out of his back pocket and wiped the sweat from his brow.

"That's a nice-looking bandanna you got there."

Lije grinned. "Felix Pierce over at the Red Palace gave it to me last night. Said it was for good luck with the Jacksonville ladies."

"Maybe you should wind it around that hat you're wearing," the marshal suggested. "It'll catch the ladies' eyes that way."

"I'll have to do that." Lije stuffed the bandanna back into his pocket. "But it's a long ways from here to Jacksonville. I'd better get started." He mounted up. "See you later, Marshal."

Lije had just passed the Red Palace Saloon when he heard Stubbs running up behind him, calling his name. He turned around and saw the marshal waving something yellow and dirty at him, and Lije stopped to let him catch up.

"You dropped this." Stubbs was puffing hard and very red in the face from his two-hundred-yard sprint. "Thought you'd want to bring your lucky bandanna along. Can't forget your good luck charm. Especially with all those road agents around. Gotta protect yourself."

Lije took the kerchief. "Much obliged, Marshal." He examined the bandanna. "But you didn't have to go to all that trouble for me."

"No trouble at all," Stubbs wheezed. "I got my own lucky piece, a rabbit's foot. I haven't been ambushed yet on my way to or from Jacksonville."

Lije grinned and said, "That's because those road agents know you never have any money with you."

They laughed and Lije took care to wind the bandanna around his hat band this time before saying good-bye once again to the marshal and riding out of town.

The chasm that was called a road wound off to the left and took a sharp drop, then rose abruptly. It wasn't considered one of the better roads to travel if you were driving a stagecoach, but a traveler on horseback could take the road at a nice easy pace.

Lije was going to take it slow during the first few miles, then speed up when he hit long, straight runs in the road. His Appaloosa was surefooted, but Lije took care not to run the horse when it wasn't necessary.

He had started early enough in the day to make it to Jacksonville well before dark. The town was twice the size of Grant's Pass. If you came in after dark, assuming you made it that far, there were always one or two unsavory characters ready to unload your gold for you before you were ready.

Lije slowed down as he approached a ravine—a good place for road agents to hide and wait for a customer. He pulled his rifle out of its saddle holster and cocked it, holding it up against his shoulder and eyeing the landscape. Lije had sharp eyes, a necessity in panning for gold. That was how he'd found the motherlode. He'd bought his stake off of a fellow who'd been panning it for over a year and had very little to show for it except a few bags of gold dust from the river. Lije had taken advantage of the miner's frustration and bought the claim for two hundred dollars, including a "long tom" and other mining equipment. A long tom was a slanted wooden trough with a pocket of mercury at the low end. Miners poured a combination of river water and silt down the trench and the mercury caught the gold dust and flakes, letting the unprofitable silt pass through.

The first few years had been hard on Lije. He'd panned the river bottom for the few bits of dust left by the former stake owner and never went into town except for supplies. He couldn't afford to spend his dwindling dust on entertainment. Then one day, he noticed that the dust was growing heavier as he moved in a new direction, leading straight to the other side of the river. There he saw a small granite rock beyond the river bed that lay sunken at the foot of a large hill. He skipped over the rest of the dust in the stream and headed straight for that rock. When he panned near it in the shallow water, he confirmed his suspicions: the dust was heavy. He was near his gold mine.

The first week, Lije made heavy use of his mining equipment. He mined so much gold out of a shallow vein that he could hardly carry it back to his horse. Now he was taking his first haul to Jacksonville. Lije wasn't happy about riding alone, but he certainly couldn't leave his gold lying around on the claim. And there was no place in Grant's Pass that he felt it would be safe. Lije was a little wary of the bank in Jacksonville, but he'd heard good things about it from other miners along the Rogue River.

He was just past the ravine and was putting away his rifle when he heard the rustle of leaves behind him to his left.

"Throw down the gold and be damned quick," a gruff voice demanded. Lije heard the familiar click of a cocked Colt and slowly untied his bag from the saddle. He didn't want to do anything that would give these bandits cause to shoot him.

As he tossed the bag down, he heard the leader instruct one of his men to pick it up. Lije had tossed the bag within his sight, hoping to get a look at one of the outlaws that might be helpful when he reported it to Henry Stubbs. A moment later, he regretted this move when the mask that hid the road agent's face slipped. Lije held his breath, hoping the thief hadn't seen the fleeting look of recognition that crossed the miner's face.

"Damn!" muttered the bandit as he pulled his mask up over the bridge of his nose. He glanced toward his victim, his eyes narrowing at the sight of the miner's controlled features. He knows I recognized him, Lije thought as he reached for his gun. The outlaw had already raised his rifle. Lije's gun was only halfway out of its holster when the first bullet caught him in the left side. He automatically drew his arm in to protect himself. With his free arm, he aimed and fired at his attacker, but missed. The second bullet caught him in the chest. It felt like a slow fire spreading in all directions and shriveling his heart in the process.

Son of a bitch was Elijah Stearns's last thought as he tumbled off his Appaloosa.

CHAPTER 2

TUCKER'S Inn was in the center of Jacksonville. It was a modest hotel for travelers, and since this was the end of winter, the heavy traffic hadn't begun yet. The man behind the desk looked like a squirrel with bifocals and ill-fitting false uppers. When Jefferson Birch walked in the front door, the little clerk's hands fluttered at the sight of the tall, dark stranger.

"May I help you, sir?" A slight quaver ran through his voice, indicating that he was expecting trouble. He no doubt got plenty of rough treatment when the weather improved and the loggers and fur traders came to town.

"Is Arthur Tisdale in his room?" Birch asked in a soft-spoken voice.

"Well, sir . . . he might be." The clerk started a flurry of activity by shuffling papers on his desk. He glanced sideways at the big, strong-jawed stranger.

Birch casually leaned over the desk. "I don't think you understood me. I asked if Arthur Tisdale is in his room. Yes or no?" Birch knew what kind of game the desk clerk was playing. It had happened often enough in larger towns. Someone who wanted to kill a man anonymously could walk into a hotel and slip the clerk a bribe for the victim's room key. This particular clerk was obviously inclined toward being paid for information.

The little man's face blanched. He said, "Room Five.

But I don't want any trouble," he warned. "I'll call the sheriff if there's any trouble."

"That's all right," Birch answered. "I'll be meeting with the sheriff later today."

Tisdale must have heard Birch's approach because he had stepped out of his room.

"Mr. Jefferson Birch?" Arthur Tisdale was a small neat man dressed in a small neat suit. His hair smelled of pomade. "I'm Arthur Tisdale of Tisdale Investigations. I'm happy to have you working for me." He held out his hand, which Birch shook, noting Tisdale's moist palm and manicure.

Birch shook his head. "I haven't said I'd take the job yet, Mr. Tisdale."

Tisdale smiled slightly. "I have confidence that you'll accept the assignment." He led the way back to the hotel lobby with Birch in tow. Birch noticed that Tisdale walked at a brisk, precise pace not uncommon to men who had spent some time in the cavalry. The desk clerk looked up at them nervously.

"Let's go across the road to the saloon," Tisdale suggested. "I'm ready for lunch."

Birch agreed. He hadn't eaten since early morning, and his breakfast had consisted mainly of hard tack and beef jerky.

In the saloon, Tisdale insisted that they order before getting down to business. Birch chose quickly, then waited while Tisdale lingered over the menu. When Arthur Tisdale got his order out of the way, he opened the conversation. "You're a long way from home, Mr. Birch. The report I received on you was from Texas. You were a Ranger there, I believe? And quite a good

one at that. Tell me, why did you leave the Rangers?"
He leaned forward, his face full of mild curiosity.

Birch wasn't used to being addressed as "Mr. Birch,"
and he didn't like to answer personal questions. "If I
refused to answer your question," he asked slowly,
"would I be jeopardizing my chance at this job?"

"Well, no, if you'd rather not tell me. I'm just curious
why a man would leave a good job like that and a fine
state like Texas to take a job with a small investigation
firm further west."

Birch was silent for a moment, then said, "No harm
in telling you, I guess. My wife died a few years ago and
I just didn't have the heart to stay. I liked my job all
right, but I wanted to move on. So here I am."

"You come highly recommended by your captain back
in the Rangers. You've been decorated several times and
I understand you're quite well-known back there. I need
someone like you for this particular job." Tisdale leaned
back expansively in his chair. "You have courage and
you're good with a gun." He took a sip of his coffee and
made a face. "Ugh! Coffee's so strong here."

Just then, the sheriff walked in. An observer could
tell he was the sheriff even without his polished tin star
because he walked with an air of authority usually
reserved to lawmen and outlaws. Tisdale waved him
over to their table.

"This is Sheriff Brent Calhoun," he said to Birch as
the sheriff joined them. "He'll fill you in on all the
details pertaining to the case." Tisdale bent to the task
of finishing his meal.

Birch knew that as head of Tisdale Investigations,
Arthur Tisdale's part was now over. He had hired the
investigator, met with the client, and put them together.
But Birch's part was just beginning.

"Mighty glad to meet you, Birch," said the Jackson County sheriff. He was a man who dispensed with formalities, settling into a more comfortable form of address. This helped Birch relax in his presence.

The sheriff continued, "We've got a spot of trouble on the road that runs from here to Grant's Pass. It's a mountain road and has always had a few road agents working the ravines, but in the past few months, robberies have increased at a staggering rate. I think that there's an organized gang out there that's getting information on who and when to rob. Miners have been killed and the stagecoach has been robbed the last three times it's carried the payroll. The loggers haven't been paid for three months."

"Has the logging camp manager hired guns to ride shotgun?"

"He's considered it. It was suggested to him by the Grant's Pass marshal, Henry Stubbs. But the logging company wants a more permanent solution. That's why I'm hiring you." The sheriff groomed his mustache absently. "Besides, would shotgun riders really solve the problem? Sooner or later they'd be ambushed as well."

Birch asked, "What makes you think these robberies are connected, maybe even organized?"

"I used to be a deputy years ago in South Dakota," Calhoun said. "I helped arrest a gang there. They were working with information supplied to them."

Birch interrupted. "The Kincaid gang."

Calhoun nodded. "It was the owner of the way station outside of Lead that was supplying Kincaid with information about the next payroll and when miners were coming through to Rapid City."

"I heard about it," Birch said. "So you were there? Tell me, Sheriff, outside of a vague idea that Jacksonville's problem might be similar to South Dakota's, do you have any other leads?"

Calhoun looked Birch straight in the eyes and shrugged slightly. "It just feels the same."

"Why isn't the marshal in Grant's Pass handling this investigation?"

Calhoun looked at Birch in surprise, then nodded, as if he'd just realized something. "I forget. You're not from around here. Do you know anything about the law in boom towns?"

Birch shook his head. "Not much."

"Well, Henry Stubbs is typical of a boom-town marshal. He keeps the town as clean as he can, but he's really in the pocket of the saloons. The saloon owners are the ones who really run Grant's Pass." Calhoun took his hat off and ran his fingers lightly around the brim. "Stubbs is close to fifty, out of shape, and practices armchair law-and-order. If he can settle a fight without lifting a finger, he'll do it."

It was Birch's turn to nod. "How many people know when the stage is making a payroll run?"

"Oh, me, my deputies, the stagecoach driver, the bank officials. I guess about a dozen people."

"So it wouldn't be too hard to figure out when to hold up the stage."

Calhoun said, "They could just send a gang member into town to watch the stage being loaded. A lone rider makes good time back to the gang and then they just have to decide when and where to ambush it."

"And what about the miners?"

"That's where you fit in. Because Grant's Pass is a boom town, unfortunately there's no bank there yet. Miners have to ride up here with their haul. In the past few months, very few miners have made it. Several have been killed on the road to Jacksonville. We don't know how the information gets to the outlaws, but it has to come from someone who lives in Grant's Pass. I'd like you to go up there and ask some questions."

Calhoun added, "Gustav Bierbohm is real interested in getting the next payroll through, otherwise the logging operation won't survive. His loggers are getting restless and several have left already. The company's offering a bonus for your cooperation."

"I'll do what I can, Sheriff."

"Then you'll take the job?"

Birch nodded. "I have a hunch that you're right about this being an organized gang."

He finished his meal, and afterward Tisdale and Calhoun walked Birch to his horse.

"You're going to ride into Grant's Pass alone?" Tisdale raised his eyebrows.

Birch turned to the sheriff. "Has anyone been ambushed on the way to Grant's Pass lately?"

Calhoun shook his head. "Come to think of it, no. Just the stagecoach."

Birch smiled slightly. "Well, then. I guess I'm better off riding in alone than taking the stagecoach. Besides, I'm not a miner." Birch tightened the cinch of his saddle before settling into its well-worn seat. He turned to Arthur Tisdale. "Any last-minute advice?"

Tisdale reached into his breast pocket and drew out something round and shiny.

"Here's your official badge, Mr. Birch. Welcome to Tisdale Investigations. I had these made up for my investigators for identification purposes."

Birch held it up. It was a circular metal badge with *Tisdale Investigations* stamped on it. Out of the corner of his eye, he caught a suppressed smile on Calhoun's face.

Suddenly, Birch was a little irritated and embarrassed by Tisdale's pompous calling card. However, he nodded solemnly to both men as he shoved the badge in his shirt pocket and rode out of town, wondering who in this rough land would bother to ask for identification before shooting.

CHAPTER 3

MARSHAL Stubbs liked to light up a cheroot after a double whiskey. He'd just come back from lunch and was sitting in one of the two chairs outside of his office when a tall, hard-jawed stranger approached him.

The marshal took out his cheroot and a match, ran his thumbnail over the match head, and drew in one end of the cheroot to light the tip.

The stranger seemed to sense that this was a ritual because he remained quiet until the cigar was going. Then he spoke. "I'm looking for Marshal Stubbs."

Stubbs replied, "He's around."

"Where can I find him?"

"Right here."

The stranger squinted at the marshal, then nodded. "I'm Jefferson Birch. I've been hired by Sheriff Calhoun to investigate the recent robberies just outside of town."

"That right? Yeah, I remember the telegram I got a few days ago. Seems like a darn fool waste of money to me. What are you going to do around here?" Stubbs eyed Birch, trying to size him up. He was lean and hard with a day's growth of whiskers on his lantern jaw. The kind of man women called handsome. His eyes were lined from squinting in the sun. They were sharp eyes. Stubbs reckoned that Birch could be a dangerous man if he were crossed.

"Oh, I plan to ask questions," Birch said coolly, "patrol the road, catch the outlaws, and collect the reward money."

"Calhoun has some idiot notion that these outlaws are a large organized gang, don't he? Damn hard to prove." Stubbs rolled the cheroot around in his mouth.

"I think the sheriff has some pretty good instincts," answered Birch. "Where can a stranger stay in Grant's Pass?"

"There's a rooming house over to the west and the Gold Hills Hotel is down the road a piece." Stubbs motioned in the direction of the hotel.

As Birch was leaving, Stubbs called out, "Birch . . ." The stranger paused and turned his head. "Check in with me when you learn something."

Birch nodded once, then headed over to the Gold Hills Hotel. Stubbs feigned sleep by pulling the brim of his hat, but he watched Jefferson Birch with a vigilant eye.

After dropping his bags off at the hotel, Birch walked over to the Rogue River Saloon & Gambling Parlor for dinner. The hotel clerk had recommended it as "the best grub you can get around these parts."

It was still early on Saturday afternoon, so there wasn't much action at the saloon. Birch had learned that the miners and loggers came in on Saturday night and spent their money at the three saloons set up in town. The Rogue River was the best of the lot. It was almost good enough to be in San Francisco.

The bar was polished redwood and a gilt-edged mirror hung over it instead of the more popular painting of a nude lady. Seated at one of the sturdy tables were three men playing cards and getting the best of the bottle. Another man leaned against the bar, cradling his own bottle and staring at the mirror with dull eyes.

"What can I do for you, stranger? Are you here to drink or just take in the view?"

She didn't look like any serving wench or saloon girl that he'd ever met. She was slender, with fiery red hair and cool blue eyes—one of the best-looking women he'd seen since he left Texas.

"Are you serving dinner now? I just got into town and I'm mighty hungry." Birch took his hat off in deference to her.

"We're serving." The woman smiled slightly and led him to a table. "Are you passing through?" The question was posed offhandedly, but Birch caught the glint of curiosity in her blue eyes. He hoped he saw a little personal interest also.

"I'll be staying here awhile," Birch said carefully. "What's fresh on your menu?"

"Rattler. Just got it in today. We also have ham of bear and venison." Then she asked, "What's your business here in town?"

"I'll have the rattler." Birch leaned back and gave her his full attention. "Is everybody in town as curious as you? By the way, you don't look like a serving girl to me. Am I getting special treatment?"

A slight smile played on her lips and she tilted her head back a bit. "I own this place, and I'm short on help right now. Nothing much happens around here, so when a stranger arrives, it'd make the front page of our newspaper—that is, if we had one. I'm sure you'll get a few more curiosity seekers, so you might as well practice on me."

Birch said, "Well, I understand that you have a clean

town here. I guess it must get dull sometimes. Maybe I can liven things up a bit."

She shook her head. "The marshal doesn't like things to get too lively. Watch your step. What do you have in mind?"

"Bring me a bottle of your best bourbon and two glasses. Then I'll tell you."

She looked dubiously at him. "Is this leading where I think it is? If so, I may have to call Shorty, my bartender, to throw you out."

Birch arched an eyebrow, suppressing the urge to chuckle. "No, ma'am. I apologize for giving you that impression. My name is Jefferson Birch. I'd like to ask you some questions about the recent robberies along the Jacksonville road."

She visibly relaxed. "Meg O'Malley, Mr. Birch. I'll bring out our best bourbon stock." She returned with a bottle of Kentucky and poured two generous glasses.

Birch swallowed some of the fiery liquid, feeling the smoothness slide down his throat and create a warm glow deep inside. "Nice place you have here."

"I've had it almost a year now. I run a clean establishment, not like some. My girls are strictly dancing girls when they're working here. What they do on their own time isn't my business. I make enough from the saloon and the tables."

"You must have made some trips to Jacksonville," Birch said, "in these past few months. Have you had any trouble on the way?"

Meg shook her head. "I take the stagecoach. And I've been very lucky. Why, the last time I was in Jacksonville, I missed the stagecoach one day by five minutes and had to stay over an extra night. The next day, I heard that it had been waylaid five miles outside of Grant's Pass."

"Was the payroll on it?"

"You mean the strongbox? Yes, I think it was. One of the drivers mentioned it. I guess I was lucky, though."

"Have any of the townspeople been ambushed on the way to Jacksonville?"

Meg shook her head. "Not that I know of. Only miners."

"How many of them have been killed?"

"Isn't that a question you should be asking Henry Stubbs?" Meg looked slightly annoyed.

"I'm asking you, though. I just want to know what you know."

She cocked her head to the side, suddenly hesitant about imparting any information to him. "I don't see how this will help you," Meg said. "But it's public knowledge. There was one miner killed a few weeks ago. His name was Elijah Stearns. Before that, I believe there were two others killed and a stagecoach driver was shot in the shoulder when he tried to reach under his seat for a rifle. That's all I know." She drained her bourbon.

"Is there anything else you can tell me about the robberies?"

"Look, Birch. I don't know what it's like where you come from, but it's not very healthy to go around asking questions as freely as you do in this town." She met his eyes squarely, an intent look passing between them. "Besides, I don't think there's a good enough reason for this investigation."

"You don't think three deaths and numerous road withdrawals are a good enough reason?" Birch raised one eyebrow.

Meg shifted uncomfortably in her chair, possibly because the topic of conversation made her wish that she were someplace else. "I'm not trying to brush aside the deaths or the robberies, but they do happen around here. It's just a part of life here in gold country."

"So you think I should leave well enough alone," Birch said pointedly, "and let the outlaws continue to terrorize the miners and shut down the logging camp."

Meg let out a sigh of frustration. She shook her head and Birch watched a bright red tendril that had escaped from the mass of pinned-up hair. She smiled and said, "No, when you put it that way, I guess not."

Birch poured them both another shot of bourbon. "I guess you were just trying to warn me."

Meg drained her glass and stood up. She gave him an arch look. "Warn you? About what? You'll probably find that most of the townspeople here aren't going to cooperate with you as freely as I have." With that, Meg got up and disappeared into the kitchen.

Birch sipped his bourbon thoughtfully. Meg O'Malley hadn't told him anything that he didn't already know. It was a discouraging start, but then Jefferson Birch was used to discouraging starts. He knew investigations took patience and an observant eye, as well as intuition and good judgment of character.

Meg soon returned with his meal, serving it to him as if she were afraid she'd have to answer more questions. It was clear to Birch that she knew something more than she was telling.

The meal was better than any meal he'd ever been served in a restaurant or saloon. He complimented Meg on the food afterward and was rewarded with a flushed look of pleasure. He learned that the green vegetable served with his rattlesnake was called asparagus and grew wild in the area. As a native of Texas, Birch's experience with vegetables was pretty much limited to potatoes and onions.

Birch watched Meg make a graceful retreat behind the bar apparently to take an inventory of the liquor supply. He couldn't take his eyes off of her and this made him feel uneasy. She was the first woman to get his attention since Audrey died two years ago. That sudden hollow feeling surfaced inside him again when he thought about his wife's death. If she and their child had lived, his son would be two years old now. He poured himself a third shot of bourbon.

CHAPTER 4

JEFFERSON Birch walked back to the hotel after dinner. He'd done a lot of thinking and come to the conclusion that the only way he'd be able to conduct his investigation was to visit the other saloons and talk to the miners and loggers. He'd been told by Tisdale, Calhoun, and Meg that several miners had been robbed. Maybe one of them had seen something and dismissed it as unimportant. Birch knew from experience that this was often the case.

He'd worked with the Rangers for almost five years, often leaving his wife alone for weeks at a time. His last assignment had been down near the Rio Grande. The captain had promised him that it would be an easy job and that Birch would be home in time for the birth of his child. Instead, he was kept at the border for over ten days, waiting for the Mexican Army to track down and bring back three escaped horse thieves who had crossed over the border. And when he returned to the small ranch that he and Audrey had built just after they were married, she and the baby had already been laid to rest. The next day, Birch resigned from the Rangers and headed for the Northwest.

Now he was working for a stuffy little man called Arthur Tisdale, a man who ran a detective agency and didn't know one end of a pistol from the other. Birch shook his head at the irony as he scraped some of the road dust off before making the rounds to all the Grant's Pass saloons.

The hotel desk clerk had been a fountain of information about the other two saloons in town. He said Stinky's was the saloon most frequented by the loggers when they weren't dancing with the girls at the Rogue River Saloon. It was a serious drinking establishment. The only entertainment was boozing, brawling, and an occasional poker game. Since the loggers were without pay for almost two months, they spent most of their time there lately.

The third saloon was called the Red Palace. It had a concert hall that always featured third-rate entertainment and hurdy-gurdy girls. This was the saloon of choice for the townspeople as well as the miners and loggers who were tired of gambling away their money at Stinky's tables and spending it on Meg's girls. The drinks were cheaper at the Red Palace and so was the entertainment.

Birch left the hotel and stepped out into the cool night air. Already the foot and horse traffic was thicker than when he'd been out earlier in the day. A few boisterous loggers stumbled down the main thoroughfare, and Birch followed them. A few doors down on the other side of the road, they entered a nondescript building. There were no signs on the outside to announce which saloon this was, but Birch suspected that it was Stinky's.

It was a darkly lit room with a rough wooden bar directly across from the entrance. A few tables were scattered around. Smoke curled and hung in the air. Raucous laughter from a table in the far corner cut through the haze. Beer and whiskey sloshed and dripped from mugs and tumblers as movement became more carefree and talk loosened up.

Birch approached the bar and ordered a large beer. It had to have been brewed locally because he knew beer didn't travel well.

Despite the fact that Birch had never met a logger before, he felt comfortable in Stinky's. The loggers minded their own business, not taking notice of strangers in their midst. As Birch cradled his beer, he noticed that quite a few men bellied up to the bar with no money. Apparently, the bar was extending credit.

Next to Birch stood a tall well-muscled man, quietly sipping White Mule and eyeing the room. He had a shock of white-blond hair and a day's growth of darker blond whiskers on his chin. He looked as if he could hoist a whole tree on his shoulder with ease. Another logger walked by him and greeted him with, "Hello, Swede."

Four men sat at a nearby table with a couple of bottles. Two of the men were having an argument. One wore a thin, scraggly beard and was missing three fingers on his right hand. The other was missing his two front teeth and his nose was misshapen, bent to one side of his face. Their voices gradually grew louder and soon Birch and everyone else in Stinky's got wind of the subject of the argument.

"Aw, hell, Stubby. Can you really expect us to believe it was so cold up North that your whiskey froze? Everyone knows that whiskey don't freeze." The man with three missing fingers scoffed.

Stubby half rose from his chair. "You calling me a liar, Fingers? It was froze pure solid. I'm telling you the truth. It was pure, one hundred percent whiskey and it was stone solid up there. Them winters up there is murder."

Fingers laughed and slapped his leg, "You really do tell the best stories, Stubby. Now sit down and shut up, will you?"

Stubby stood frozen for a moment, like the mythical whiskey. The other two drinking partners sensed that something was about to happen and moved slightly away from the table. Suddenly, Stubby upended it and dove for Fingers, fists flying. One thing led to another and before he knew it, Birch was in the middle of a rough-and-tumble brawl. Around the room, logger after logger joined in the fray.

Birch had just picked up his beer when a stranger's fist aimed straight for his face, intent on getting Birch involved in the growing fracas. Birch's free hand was hooked on his gunbelt, so he did the next best thing to defending himself: he ducked. When the blow didn't graze his head, he looked up and saw Swede's powerful hand curled around the stranger's now immobile arm. Birch set his beer down with deliberate care, then hauled off with a right to the unknown logger's jaw. A moment later, he spotted the same logger swinging away at another brawler. Birch turned in time to deflect an airborne chair aimed at Swede's head. The big man nodded a silent thank-you to Birch.

He noticed that the loggers didn't pull out any knives or guns during the fight. It almost seemed that there were certain rules to follow during a logger's brawl. Fighting appeared to loosen them up after a day of cutting and hauling logs. However, since Birch couldn't hold an intelligent conversation with brawling loggers and he wasn't being paid to get beaten up, he made his way to the door, dodging flying fists and furniture. A massive hand reached past him and gave the door a mighty shove. Outside, and after a few deep breaths of the clear night air, Birch saw that the hand belonged to Swede.

"You're a little puny to be a logger, but you held your own in there," Swede said mildly. "Some of those boys come to town just to booze and brawl. There's nothing personal in it, it's just their way of having fun. But you look like a man who picks his fights carefully."

Birch nodded. "The name's Jefferson Birch. I heard someone in there call you Swede."

Swede laughed good-naturedly. "I was born in Norway, but those fellows don't know Sweden from Norway, so I tolerate the nickname."

"I see," Birch said in a wry tone of voice.

"What's your business in town?" Swede asked, then added, "You don't look like a miner, either. You dress better."

"I'm investigating the Jacksonville road robberies and the related deaths of the miners."

Swede laughed. "Maybe you can prevent another payroll withdrawal. The logging company sure would appreciate it. Gustav Bierbohm, too."

"The logging camp manager?"

Swede nodded. His forehead wrinkled, probably at the thought of another month without pay. "I think all the loggers would like to get their pay—and two months' back pay. We don't like to work for nothing."

"Why don't you leave?"

Swede shook his head. "A lot of us might if we had any money. But Bierbohm is fair and it really isn't his fault that he's had a bad streak of luck. Besides, he pays well when the money gets through. But if this continues, I'm sure that some of the fellows will drift away."

Birch offered to buy Swede a drink, so they headed over to the Rogue River Saloon.

"You're going to have a lot of work ahead of you, Birch. I wouldn't even know where to start."

"Why do you say that?"

"There are probably more than a couple of outlaws working that road," Swede said. "There could be several gangs."

"There's a possibility that this is all one large organized gang, Swede. The robberies have increased in frequency over the past few months. It's possible that someone here in town leaks information to road agents when a miner goes to Jacksonville with gold in his pocket or when a payroll comes here."

Swede shook his head in disbelief as they neared their destination. "Let me know if you need any help. I'm sure I could round up a few fellows if you need them."

Meg's saloon was brightly lit and gay with music and laughter. Dancing girls hung on the arms of the more successful miners and sipped weak tea in place of the expensive drinks that the hapless miners ordered for them. The gambling tables were in the back, crowded with men who were sure that their luck would change. A miner with pockets lined with gold dust could try his luck at the faro, blackjack, and monte tables, if he were so inclined. A roulette wheel was spinning and clacking away while several men played poker at another table. In the midst of it all, Meg O'Malley surveyed her domain with a sharp eye out for the dishonest croupier or the disgruntled customer.

She was wearing a red velvet dress with a daring neckline this evening. Jet black beads and brocade decorated the bodice and sleeves. With her fine red hair piled high and her sparkling necklace and earrings, she was the center of attention everywhere she went. Every man desired her. Jefferson Birch was no exception.

Meg glided over, her eyes fastened on him. The rich scent of her perfume intoxicated the customers, causing many to lose their concentration.

"Mr. Birch! I didn't think you would be back this evening. I expected that you would be out asking questions, or perhaps drinking in one of the other places in town." She smiled into his eyes as she spoke. Birch fancied he saw a faint blush on her cheeks, but tried to dismiss it as a reflection of her red dress.

He smiled. "I was at Stinky's, but it became too . . . active."

Meg noticed Swede for the first time. "And are you going to introduce us?"

The logger spoke for himself. "I am called Swede." He bowed slightly.

"But gentlemen! You don't have drinks in your hands." She looked genuinely distressed at this revelation. "The first drink is on the house." Meg signaled the bartender and another bottle of Kentucky bourbon appeared. "Enjoy yourselves, Mr. Birch, Mr. . . . Swede." She moved away to tend to her other customers.

"I haven't been here very much because I'm saving most of my wages to bring my wife Greta over here," Swede explained. "That's why I go to Stinky's. The beer is cheaper."

"Yeah, this place would tempt a saint," Birch replied. He watched Meg move from table to table as the two of them drank. Swede talked about his wife and their plans to move back to the prairie, build a farm, and raise crops. Then he finished his drink and got up. "I'd better get back to camp now, Birch. I'll see you there when you come around to talk to Bierbohm."

Birch nodded after the tall Norwegian. From his vantage point, Birch could see most of the room. The gambling tables were at the back, to his left. The entrance was on his right and straight ahead was the dancing area. A lively waltz was being played by a fiddler and an accompanying pianist. The dance floor was crowded with energetic miners ready to spend their gold dust on a pretty girl, if she'd put up with aching arches and tender toes. While he was enjoying the music and watching the dancing, Birch saw out of the corner of his eye a man pull a gun on the croupier at the blackjack table.

CHAPTER 5

THERE were many hazards that Meg O'Malley endured every night. Fights broke out, dealers tried to cheat customers and skim off the top, and drunks tried to paw her with sweaty hands while whispering slurred endearments with breath that would be hazardous near an open flame. Despite these irritations, Meg loved running the Rogue River Saloon. She certainly made enough money to hire someone else to oversee the hired help and greet customers, but Meg enjoyed the laughter, the music, the smoky atmosphere, and the gaiety that pervaded the saloon every night.

When she had first bought the Rogue River Saloon, the townspeople had been a little worried that she might not be able to run it properly. After all, she obviously came from East Coast wealth. What did she know about running a saloon? Could she handle the fights, the drunks, and the rowdys?

She soon proved that she was more than just a fiery beauty, she was also a competent manager. Not only did she run the saloon with energetic efficiency, but she added a gambling parlor in the back for those men who wished to part with their dust doubly quick. By the end of her first year in Grant's Pass, Meg had proven, without a doubt, that she was a smart businesswoman and a solid citizen.

She heard Shorty, the bartender, call to her from the far end of the bar. Despite his nickname, he was a big, beefy man who served as a bouncer when customers became obnoxious. He'd been with Meg since she'd taken over the saloon and she trusted his instincts. He usually could sense when a fight was going to start and do something about it before it became too heated.

She moved toward him and he gestured at the gaming tables. "Over there. It's Stone again." Meg looked over at the blackjack table and saw her dealer's face stiffen as Luke Stone, an angry dark-haired patron, drew a gun. Stone used to preach in her saloon on Sundays, and was polite and soft-spoken when he was sober. But he'd get mean and pick fights when he had a few drinks in him.

Meg said, "I'd better handle this one, Shorty." She sighed and started toward the trouble.

"Need any help?" Shorty rested his large hand on the scattergun he kept behind the bar.

"I don't think so, but keep an eye on me."

When she reached the table, Stone was swaying dangerously from side to side. He took a swig from the nearly empty bottle of rye sitting in front of him.

"You lousy stinking dealer!" Stone slurred loudly. "You've been cheating me and everyone else. I saw you dealing from the bottom of the deck. We all did." He looked around at the other customers for support. They avoided his gaze, neither supporting nor denying his accusation. Either stand could result in a bullet.

The dealer, John, kept his hands in sight, but he was pale. A hush fell over the saloon. The music died and both drinking and dancing customers seemed as if they were suspended in midair.

"Miss O'Malley don't let us cheat the customers, sir," John tried to calm the miner down. "She'd have my hide."

"I run a clean operation," Meg said from behind the disoriented customer.

He turned unsteadily and narrowed his eyes at her.

She smiled, but she was seething inside. There were some nights she wished she didn't have to be such a lady. "I'm sure we can settle this elsewhere, Mr. Stone," she cooed.

He tried to focus his eyes on her. "Miss O'Malley?"

"Let's not disturb the rest of the customers, shall we? We can go over to my corner table and talk this out. I think the rest of these people would like to continue the game, Mr. Stone."

Meg ushered him to her private table in the back of the saloon. She flicked her wrist toward the musicians and dealers, indicating that they should go on about their business. A moment later, music filtered through the saloon and dealers were calling out to players to place their bets. The customers ordered more whiskey as if nothing had happened.

While she was slipping into her chair, Meg withdrew a small dagger from the pocket of her voluminous skirt and kept it hidden from view, but easily accessible. She turned to Luke Stone. "Now Mr. Stone, what is the problem?"

"Ain't no problem. I just want to get my money back. Your dealer was cheating me. I brought three ounces of gold dust to this place and now I'm almost broke. What'll my wife and kids say?" He looked miserably at a spot on the table.

"That's what happens when you gamble, Mr. Stone. Sometimes the house wins, sometimes you win. You knew that when you came in here." Meg wanted to be sympathetic. She certainly felt sorry for his wife and children, but if she gave everyone their money back when they came in with a hard luck story, she'd soon be out of business.

Stone leaned over the table in desperation, squinting drunkenly and leering at Meg's bosom. She found herself flushing under Luke Stone's hungry gaze, but she told herself that he was trying to intimidate her and she stood her ground.

He arose and lurched toward her, across the table. Meg always sat with her back to the wall, a habit she'd acquired when working in bigger cities, and she suddenly found herself trapped between the wall, the table, and the chair. Then a hand clamped down on Stone's shoulder and spun him around. Jefferson Birch's fist connected with Stone's jaw. The miner staggered back from the blow and landed on a nearby table, disrupting a poker game.

For a moment she was pleased that Birch had come to her aid, but her feelings quickly changed to anger.

The poker players were disgruntled over having their table upended and their cards and ante scattered around the floor. One of the men had Stone by the collar and was saying, "Why you, I oughta . . ."

Stone, looking a little more sober from Birch's punch, pointed a finger at Birch and said, "He's the one who started it."

Meg fumed at the scene that had escalated from Birch's interference. She watched the other three players slowly stand up, keeping their eyes on Birch. One of the men addressed Birch. "What's the meaning of this?"

One of the other cardplayers made a move for his gun. Meg knew her dagger wouldn't do any good and she shrank against the wall. She saw Shorty reaching for his scattergun, ready to disperse any trouble. She made a mental note to buy a small derringer if she came out of this situation unscathed.

Birch calmly unsnapped his holster and hooked his hand casually on his gunbelt. Uncertainty crept into the face of the cardplayer whose hand hovered by his gun.

Birch said, "If I draw, I shoot, so I'd be obliged if you'd take your hand away from that gun. I was only protecting Miss O'Malley."

There was a tense moment, then it passed. As the men backed away slowly, picking up their money, chips, and gold dust, Meg heard one of the men muttering under his breath, "Since when did Meg O'Malley ever need this kind of protection?" She furrowed her brow in irritation.

Meg approached Birch, who cocked his head slightly as he asked, "Are you all right?"

Stifling her anger, she motioned for him to go to her private table. After they sat down, she said, "Mr. Birch, I appreciate what you just did . . ." She paused, then added, "In a way. I know you meant to do the right thing and for that, I must thank you. However, I could have handled the situation very well by myself. And if there had been any further trouble, I always can depend on Shorty."

"Yes, I got a glimpse of that dagger of yours. I'm sure it would have left a nice souvenir scar on Mr. Stone."

Meg was silent for a moment. "If you knew that I was handling the situation, why did you interfere?"

"Well, I thought that Mr. Stone wouldn't have appreciated the scar when he woke up the next morning. A fist does the same job without the mess."

"Mr. Birch, I don't appreciate men coming to my rescue in my own saloon," Meg said in an icy tone. "It doesn't look good. Customers begin to lose confidence

in my ability to run a proper gambling establishment if
I get help from another customer."

Birch stood up. "Then I apologize for undermining
your authority, Miss O'Malley."

Meg wondered if he'd taken offense to her lambast-
ing. She suddenly felt apologetic. "Mr. Birch, I'm sorry
if I sound ungrateful and shrewish. I know that you
only did what comes naturally to you because you are a
gentleman." She laughed. "And there are so few of
those around here. I hope you understand my
position."

He nodded, his face softening as a slight smile crept
across his features. "I'll be more careful to contain my
rescue attempts to outside your establishment, Miss
O'Malley. May I make it up to you by taking you out
tomorrow afternoon, perhaps for a buggy ride?"

She hesitated at first, but decided that it couldn't hurt
her reputation any further. She nodded. "Thank you. I
would enjoy that, Mr. Birch. You may call for me at two
o'clock tomorrow."

She watched him leave, the saloon doors swinging
closed behind him, and wondered what she was letting
herself in for.

CHAPTER 6

SUNDAY was hot, dry, and quiet. Most of the townspeople were at church early in the morning, and except for those who wanted to save their souls, most of the miners were back at their claims.

Birch walked through the empty thoroughfare toward the church. He hoped to get something to eat while he was there, having learned from the desk clerk that his soul could be ministered to while he ate a hearty breakfast at the Red Palace on the edge of town. It was aptly named. The face of the big barnlike building was painted red. Above the door was a shakily hand-lettered sign with a crude picture of a man and woman dancing while a fiddler leered at them.

Inside the hurdy-gurdy palace, the tables and bar were rough hewn wood. The crowd looked no different from any Saturday night crowd. Miners and loggers elbowed their way to the bar and ordered rye or whiskey as if they were trying to cleanse more than their souls. Dancing girls sidled up to temporarily wealthy men and seduced them into buying another drink. A sheet hung on the wall behind the bar, probably covering up some barroom painting of a nude lady. The rough wooden platform that served as a stage for entertainers was bare, except for a makeshift pulpit in the center and a familiar figure turning pages in a Bible. It was the miner from last night, Luke Stone. He was wearing a somber black coat.

Birch sat at a table and gave the serving girl his order.
She scurried away quickly to fill it just as the Reverend
Stone began his sermon: "Friends, we must repent our
evil ways. Gold is the demon of the soul and we must
recognize the evil power it has over us. And we must
fight it with all our strength. When you hold that gold
dust in your hand, do you feel a lustful joy come over
you? Do you feel that power coursing through your
being?"

The reverend took a swig of rye from a bottle conven-
iently placed under the pulpit. The miners roared in
agreement.

"Friends, we have a problem here in Grant's Pass. This
problem punishes us for our own wretched greed and
misery. We cannot leave this town without fear of being
accosted by sinners, thieves, and murderers. And why is
that? Does it happen for no reason? No! I say no! It
happens because *we* are the thieves and murderers, *we*
rob the land out of greed for gold. *We* sell our souls for
that pound of dust. There is a fear, yes."

He took another long pull from his rye before
continuing.

"But it is a fear not only for our worldly possessions,
but a fear for our mortal souls."

By the time Birch's meal arrived, the Reverend Stone
was working the crowd up to a frenzy over the loss of
the miners' lives as well as the loss of the gold.

The reverend finished his sermon just about the time
Birch finished his meal. Stone left his pulpit and came
over to Birch's table. Birch drew back from his table a
bit, in case Stone's intentions were to fight.

"You're Birch, the man who hit me last night," Stone
said. The tone of his voice didn't hold any animosity.

"You were accosting Miss O'Malley," Birch stated

evenly. "It was my duty to protect her from your advances."

Stone seemed satisfied with Birch's explanation. "Well, I just want to thank you for that. I was mighty inebriated last night and you thrashed me soundly for my evil ways. I am repenting."

He touched the bruise on his left jaw slightly as if to remind himself that Birch could be a dangerous man. "I have no wish to make trouble. I just wanted to ask you what you're doing here in town. You're not a prospector from the looks of you. I'd say you don't have the build of a logger either."

"I'm here on business. I'm looking for those thieves and murderers you were preaching about earlier."

Stone smirked. "The miners like to hear that on a Sunday. It takes away some of the guilt they might feel about abandoning their wives and children or swindling someone into buying a salted gold mine. And every time they hear about the death of a miner, they feel vindicated. It takes their minds off being afraid *they'll* be robbed on the road to Jacksonville."

Stone paused. "Come to think of it," he continued, "I don't think there's been a successful run to Jacksonville with gold for a few months. If those robbers aren't careful, they could turn this into a ghost town before all the gold has been mined."

Birch nodded thoughtfully. "But I doubt that outlaws care if Grant's Pass becomes a ghost town before its time. If Grant's Pass dries up, they'll just move on to another area."

Birch leaned forward and asked, "You're a miner. Don't you ever fear for your safety? Don't you wonder where you'll end up if this town closes down because of those robberies?"

Stone's laugh was more like a bark. "That's why I drink."

Birch sized up the reverend. "What about anger—don't the miners ever get angry and talk about banding together to find out who's threatening their livelihood?"

Stone shook his head sadly. "Mister, you don't know nothing about miners. You haven't been struck by gold fever, have you?"

Birch slowly shook his head.

Stone continued, "Well, it's like no other feeling in the world. You become obsessed with finding that yellow metal. You work it, you live it, you dream it. It's always in your thoughts. Whether you're drinking or with your woman, the thought of finding more gold is never out of your mind. Working a stake is like being married to a beautiful woman—you begin to think that every man who comes within a stone's throw of your property is trying to horn in on your claim. So you become careful and secretive. You trust no one."

"So you're saying," Birch summed up, "that the miners can't get together long enough to drive those outlaws away."

"That's what I'm saying. It's funny, too," Stone reflected with a small smile, "because most of the miners have set up camp near each other. We've almost become a community with all the hardships that we endure."

"Then it should be easy to call a meeting and work together to get rid of the outlaws or at least to protect yourselves."

Stone shook his head. "You don't understand. Miners may live together, but I'd say the one reason that binds us together is distrust. It's easier to keep an eye on the other fellow when he's sleeping in the tent next to you." He stood up. "Most of them are secretly glad to hear that another miner has been killed. It's just more stake for the rest of us. You should see them hover over the abandoned claim like vultures," the reverend said with distaste. "Why don't you come by the camp tonight? You could meet some of them and find out for yourself. You might even pick up some helpful information, although it would only be by a slip of the tongue if you did."

Birch agreed and watched Stone weave his way out of the saloon. He might be a drunk, Birch thought, but he seemed to be an honest man when he was sober.

After a few questions, Birch located the owner of the Red Palace, Felix Pierce. He was a dapper man of medium height and wore plenty of pomade in his graying hair. Even his mustache gleamed with the scented ointment. He wore a brocade vest, pocketwatch, and snakeskin boots. Birch took an immediate dislike to him, but he controlled his expression so it wouldn't be apparent.

"Mr. Pierce?" Birch extended his hand. "My name is Jefferson Birch."

Felix Pierce listened to Birch's introduction with a blank expression on his face. Pierce had gambler's eyes, the kind of eyes that knew how to hide the excitement of an inside straight. After considering Birch's proffered hand, he shook it firmly.

"What can I do for you, Mr. Birch?" he asked. Birch noticed that for a man who wore fancy vests and boots, he had a powerful voice. Birch always expected Pierce's type to be all show and no go when it came to facing off with him. Pierce's tone held a hint of threat, but Birch wasted no time in getting down to business.

"Well, you may have heard about my interest in the robberies that have taken place along the road to Jacksonville," Birch began, hating himself for the lie that followed. "I'll be talking to most of the business owners here in Grant's Pass and Meg O'Malley suggested that I talk to you."

Felix Pierce gestured to a table and they sat down. He leaned back in his chair and crossed his arms. "So Meg suggested that you talk to me, huh?"

"Yes. She said that if anyone knew about these robberies, you would."

Pierce stared darkly at Birch for a moment, then suddenly threw his head back and laughed mirthlessly. "Oh she did, did she?" When he stopped chuckling he leaned forward, placing his hands on the table. "I suggest that Meg didn't say any such thing. Why would I know anything about the robberies, except that they're bad for business? I've been doling out credit to almost every customer who comes in here, and if I could find the miserable wretches responsible for these robberies, I'd take my pair of mother-of-pearl six-shooters and plug every single blessed one of them."

"So you're saying that you have no information on the road withdrawals?" Birch played dumb around men like Pierce because it put them off their guard. "No one's come in for a drink after being robbed and said something that may have been significant?"

Pierce looked at Birch levelly. Birch could tell his ploy wasn't working. "No. No one has come in after being robbed and described the outlaws to me," Pierce said in a sarcastic tone. "Now, if you're going to buy a drink, you may stay in my bar. If you're just going to bother the customers, I'm going to have to ask you to leave. As for Meg O'Malley, she would never have told you that I knew something about those robberies when she knows quite well that I don't."

Birch shrugged and smiled congenially. "Can't blame a man for trying."

"Now if you'll excuse me, I have to meet someone."

Pierce got up abruptly, signaling the bartender that Birch might be trouble. It was a subtle sign, but Birch knew what it meant. He decided to buy a drink.

While Birch waited for his whiskey, he sauntered around the saloon, trying to strike up conversations with some of the other patrons. One man, his tongue loosened by the bottle, started to respond, but a glance in the direction of the bar sobered him up quickly. He offered a muttered excuse to Birch and left the saloon. Birch went back to his table and sat down.

Just after his drink appeared, a rangy redheaded youth sauntered up to his table.

"Name's Deputy Carver," the youth said, puffing out his chest. "I hear you been bothering Mr. Pierce and most of the patrons with questions."

Not wanting to get up from his chair, Birch settled for looking up into the acne-scarred face and small, mean eyes of Deputy Carver.

"Mr. Pierce and I have already had our discussion. I'm just sitting here quiet now and having a whiskey."

Carver took a step back and fixed Birch with a grim stare. "I'm gonna ask you nice only once, then I'll have to get rough." He unbuckled the gun at his left hip.

A hush fell over the saloon.

Birch slowly raised his glass and drained half of the whiskey. He was damned if this puppy was going to order him around. With one deft movement, Jefferson sent his table careening into the deputy's left side. Carver let out a yelp and stumbled backward, losing his balance and his dignity at the same time. Before he could dust himself off, Birch rose from his seat.

Pierce's authoritative voice called out from the back of the saloon, "What's going on here?" The saloon owner was quickly at Birch's side. Pierce took in the scene before him: Carver sprawled out on the floor and Birch standing over him.

He looked sharply at Birch and barked, "What's the meaning of this?"

Birch replied, "This young deputy here tried to throw me out. He said that I was disturbing the peace, but I was just having a quiet drink."

A humiliated Carver was now standing and brushing himself off. He threw Birch a sullen look, then turned to explain his presence to Felix Pierce.

"I was just doing my job," the deputy said, chagrined. "This here fellow is trouble. I was doing you a favor, Mr. Pierce. After all, I am the law."

Birch cut in. "Sheriff Calhoun gave me a job to do and I aim to do it. Now, your boss, Marshal Stubbs, is being real cooperative. Why don't you go run back to him and talk to him. He'll tell you it's not your job to bother a citizen when he's just having a quiet drink and making polite conversation."

Pierce took a deep breath and said to Carver, "Jim, I know what you're trying to do, but you're going to get yourself and the marshal in trouble if you go throwing your weight around here. Birch is right. You can't roust a fellow out of a saloon just because he was talking to a few customers."

"But I heard what he said about asking questions around town and I just wanted to . . ."

"Jim, enough!" Pierce said in a rough tone. "Just go about your business and leave Mr. Birch alone. You can't throw someone in the pokey for asking questions, especially when he's asking questions about the robberies."

Birch thought he detected a note of warning as Pierce told the deputy, "You know it's not like we have anything to hide. We just don't know anything."

Jim Carver's face grew red with the added indignity of being reprimanded for his actions. "But Mr. Pierce . . ."

"Deputy," Pierce said, eyes flashing, "go on about your business."

Carver was trembling with suppressed rage. "Don't think you've seen the last of me, Birch. I'll be watching you close and the moment you step out of line, I'll be there."

Then he turned and left.

Pierce was still there. "He can be quite a hothead. I'd watch my step if I were you, Mr. Birch."

"Why are you suddenly so concerned for my welfare, Pierce?"

Felix Pierce raised his eyebrows slightly. "I'm not interested in you specifically. I just don't like trouble in this town. Marshal Stubbs keeps the town clean, sometimes despite his young deputy. Besides, I don't like to attend funerals," Pierce paused here, then looked emphatically at Birch, "even the funerals of strangers." With that, he walked away.

Birch looked around for his drink and realized that it had upended with the table he had rammed into the deputy. He considered ordering another one, then remembered that he was supposed to meet Meg in front of her saloon.

CHAPTER 7

BIRCH found Meg waiting for him when he drove up to the Rogue River Saloon in the rented buggy. It was a two-seater with spindly wheels drawn by a high-spirited horse called Devil. The springs beneath the seat were taut, making the buggy ride a jolting experience when it was taken at a pace faster than an easy trot.

Meg wore a soft green riding dress. She'd let her hair fall loose around her shoulders for the afternoon and it caught the midday sun's rays, highlighting her red strands. As Birch helped her into the buggy, he caught a whiff of her sweet perfume.

"Where should we go?" Meg asked, busily arranging a basket full of food that she'd brought along.

"Well, you know the area better than I do," Birch pointed out. "Which way?"

"Let's go south out of town. We can get to the river if we take Dead Indian Pass a few miles outside of Grant's Pass."

As they headed out, Birch noticed the marshal sitting in his usual spot in the chair outside the jailhouse. Stubbs waved Birch down.

Birch turned to Meg. "Excuse me for a minute, Meg."

She nodded and he pulled the rig over. He got down, tied the buggy to a hitching post just beyond the jailhouse, and walked over to the marshal. Birch had thought he saw a hint of fear and dislike in Meg's face when Henry Stubbs waved them down. As he approached the marshal, he wondered what it could be that made Meg look with such disdain at the town's law-and-order.

Stubbs was sucking on a cheroot. He smiled and said, "Afternoon, Birch."

"Afternoon, Marshal."

"Nice day for a picnic—especially with that little filly you've got over there." The marshal's eyes fixed on Meg, who was sitting patiently in the buggy. "That there's a fine figure of a woman."

Birch wanted him to get to the point. He was in no mood to hear Stubbs rhapsodizing over Meg's figure. "You didn't call me over here to talk about Miss O'Malley's virtues, Marshal. What can I do for you?"

Stubbs turned his attention to Birch and said, "I hear you had a little disagreement with my deputy this morning."

Birch nodded shortly. "It wasn't a very friendly introduction."

Stubbs stood up to stretch, his massive bulldog body straining at his shirt. The effect was not lost on Birch, who was not anxious to have Stubbs on his bad side.

"Jim can lose his temper easily." Stubbs shook his head. "And when the boy takes a dislike to someone, I sometimes wonder what goes through his head. I just want to apologize for his behavior, Birch."

The ex-Ranger accepted the apology. "But why does a boy like that have a deputy's job?"

Stubbs sat down again, as if standing had been too much work for him. "Well, son, I've been hoping he'd grow out of his hotheadedness. Maybe I was wrong, but I think he'll make a mighty fine lawman once he gets hold of his temper some."

Birch couldn't see it happening, but then, Birch had

only just met Jim Carver. Stubbs was in a better position to judge, he decided.

Stubbs grinned and said, "I hear you got into two fistfights last night. You don't waste any time, do you, son?"

"That fight at Stinky's started with someone else and I got out of there as soon as it started. There was no fight at the Rogue River Saloon, I just prevented a drunk from assaulting Miss O'Malley." Birch stared impassively at the marshal. "Now is there anything else?"

Stubbs shook his head. "Naw. Just wanted to talk to you for a moment and tell you I'm sorry about my deputy. I told him to stop bothering you."

At this point, Carver strolled up to the jailhouse and threw a glare in Birch's direction. Birch returned the deputy's glare with a hard stare of his own.

Stubbs noticed the deputy and addressed him. "Jim, I was just telling Mr. Birch here that we had a little talk earlier and you won't be bothering him again, will you?"

The deputy said smugly, "I was just doing my job, Marshal."

Birch smiled coldly and said to Carver, "You act like I'm the enemy, Deputy. If you continue to interfere with my investigation here, I might suspect you of something."

The deputy scowled. "Think what you like, but watch your step. I don't have to answer to you, Birch. And I don't like your investigation. It just stirs up trouble— you can tell that to Sheriff Calhoun."

Stubbs looked darkly at his deputy and spoke in a sharp tone. "That's enough, Jim. Just avoid Birch here for the next few days. If you don't watch your step, you'll have to answer to me."

When Birch was a Ranger, he'd had a few superior

officers tell him that they didn't like his method of investigating. But he always got results, so the grumbling usually went away. In this case, he was faced with several ways of dealing with Carver: he could go to Arthur Tisdale with the problem and probably spend months working on a solution; he could go directly to Sheriff Calhoun and complain, and probably spend days or weeks working out the problem with him; or he could solve it himself. He chose the latter.

"What the marshal says makes sense, Carver," Birch said. "You stay away from me while I'm here and everyone will be happy."

Carver looked frustrated. He turned to Stubbs. "But Marshal, we can't just . . ." The deputy trailed off, suddenly aware of Stubbs's stony eyes on him. He turned a hate-filled glare onto Birch. "Okay, but I'll be keeping an eye out and if you step out of line or get into trouble, I'll be there."

Birch ignored his empty threats and turned to Stubbs. "Well, Marshal, if there's nothing else . . ."

Birch turned to go. He was aware of the deputy's mean, spiteful gaze following him until he and Meg were well out of sight.

The country turned into great pine forests that rose up the sides of mountains, blue-green trees reaching up and stretching out for miles, broken only by occasional small areas where the trees had been harvested. The effect was spectacular and both Meg and Birch rode in awed silence for a time.

Finally Birch spoke what was on his mind. "You haven't asked me anything about the meeting I had with the marshal back there."

Meg smiled and smoothed her skirt. "I heard some of it."

"I got the feeling Marshal Stubbs was hiding something. His deputy isn't very subtle."

Meg laughed. "I could hear everything Jim had to say from where I was. The whole town could hear him, I'm sure." She sobered suddenly and added, "Of course, you should be warned that Carver is a dangerous man."

" 'Boy' is more like it, Meg. He's a boy doing a man's job."

Meg shook her head slightly. "But he's easily angered and impulsive. That's a dangerous combination, even for a young boy."

Birch thought about it for a minute and agreed. "Especially for a young boy. Consider me warned, Meg." After a moment, Birch added, with a slight smile, "A woman with a dagger is also a dangerous combination."

Meg's cheeks flushed. "I kept it well-hidden. I don't know how you spotted it."

"I'm trained to notice things like that. But I don't think any of your customers noticed it."

"I'm sure if they had," Meg observed, "they would have cheered me on. Most of them were so inebriated by then that they would consider a fight to be good sport."

Birch chuckled at the thought.

"What else did you notice about me?" she asked.

Birch turned to look at Meg and raised his eyebrows. "What do you mean?"

She persisted. "What sort of things are you trained to notice? Take me, for example."

Birch took a moment to answer. "Well, right now you might be wondering whether I've telegraphed for information on your past. In fact, that might be one of the reasons you agreed yesterday to go on this outing with me."

Meg's sharp look at him confirmed what he'd only guessed at. He modestly explained as he glanced rapidly down at her lap, "I saw your hands twisting and fidgeting earlier, so I guessed you were nervous about something."

Meg turned away, but not before Birch got a brief look at the range of emotions that swept across her face.

He added, "But as long as you're not involved in the road robberies and you're telling me the truth about what you know, I have no reason to check your background. I believe that a man's or woman's past is their own business." Birch fell into a silence broken only by the sounds of the squeaky springs and wheels turning on the rutted road.

After a few minutes, he said, "Actually, I don't need to wire anywhere to be able to tell that you've been educated in a fancy finishing school, probably back east in New York."

"Boston, actually." Her tone was rigid.

They continued on in silence. Birch could sense Meg's stiffness next to him as their buggy jolted over the stony path.

After a few minutes, he felt her hand touch his arm. "I'm sorry. I had no right to be angry with you when you only answered my question. Please, go on. What else can you tell about my dreadful past."

Birch shook his head slowly. "I think it would be better if we changed the subject."

Meg tried again. "No, please. It just took me by surprise. I thought I'd shed my Boston-bred background, but you recognized it in me. What else did you notice?"

Birch sighed. "You've been married before as well. It must have been a painful memory." He went on to explain. "It's your way with men. A woman who had never married wouldn't have handled that miner with such confidence last night. As for your good breeding, you once emphasized to me that your dancing girls were employed just for that purpose, as if it mattered what I thought of you. Only a person with good breeding would care what people thought of her here in the West."

Meg nodded thoughtfully. "I come from a very wealthy family. Back then, I never thought my life would take such a dramatic turn." She interrupted her confession by pointing out the turn in the path. "That's Dead Indian Pass to the left. It's very short and takes us right to the river."

"What would happen if we went to the right?"

"We'd get there eventually, but we'd have to go through the mining camp. It would also take us further up the river where the miners pan."

Birch made a note for his return trip to the miner's camp that evening.

For the rest of the trip, she told him how she had fallen in love with the gardener's son. He had been her childhood playmate, but as they grew older, Meg's family discouraged their friendship. Her parents, in all their wisdom, wanted her to meet the eligible young men in Boston society and marry someone who would meet their approval.

"All I wanted was David," she said. "He tried to talk sense into me, reminding me of our different backgrounds, but I didn't care. Finally, he had to admit that he loved me, too. We ran away, heading west. For two years, we moved around, finally settling in New Orleans. But a few months after we were settled and he'd gotten work, he was killed."

Birch said, "You could have gone back to your family."

"No." She turned her face away. "The man who murdered David was my brother. I wouldn't go back with him." Meg turned back to Birch, her chin set determinedly. "Jerome, my brother, tried to take me back. He'd been in New Orleans on business and ran into David at the bank where my husband worked as a teller. I'm not sure how it happened, but they got into a fistfight. David went down and struck his head on a table edge. Jerome was cleared of murder, but in my eyes . . ."

Her voice drifted off and she shook her head slightly.

"I worked my way out here. My father sent money to me before I left New Orleans"—she broke off with a laugh—"I think in his mind he was trying to compensate me for my loss, and hoped I would reconcile with them, but I took the money and moved further away. I used most of it to buy the saloon."

They came to a spot that had shade trees and a satiny green area to lay the lunch items out. A weeping willow hung over the river, trailing lacy green branches in the water. The willow's trunk was just far enough back from the bank to sit under without getting Meg's skirts damp.

She had prepared a lunch of cold chicken, a loaf of crusty bread, and a bottle of wine. It reminded Birch of the times when he and Audrey would take the wagon out to a river like the Rogue and spend the day sitting in the shade of a tree or going for a long walk. She would always include his favorite, an oatcake. He could almost smell it now. He accepted the glass of wine that Meg offered him and for a moment almost called her by his wife's name.

"You were off somewhere for a while," Meg observed.

"Just thinking about Texas." It sounded bleak after Meg's reluctant and painful monologue. But unlike

Meg, Birch didn't feel the need to unburden himself to anyone. Not yet.

They talked instead about the town and the people Meg knew. She offered insights about some of the citizens that would have taken him several weeks to pick up. At one point, he asked her if anyone did anything unusual in town.

"Well, Minnie Perkins, the dry goods' store owner's wife, went swimming last week with the town doctor, Jacob Stanford. Rumor has it that they got drunk together, took off all their clothes, and jumped into the Rogue. I don't imagine that's the sort of unusual action you want, though."

Birch chuckled. "No, but it sounds interesting. What I want to know is if someone in town is making regular trips out of town—or even just mysteriously disappearing for a short length of time, a day or two."

She thought for a moment. "Lots of people disappear from time to time. I don't keep track of them all . . . wait a minute. Felix Pierce goes out of town for supplies at odd times."

"What do you mean at odd times?"

"Well, I've noticed that he'll take an empty wagon with him on his trips to Jacksonville to pick up supplies that have supposedly been delivered, but several times he's come back with an empty wagon as well. I don't know if it means anything, though. I asked him once about bringing an empty wagon back and he explained that the delivery had been delayed reaching Jacksonville by three days and he thought it would be better to come on back home rather than to stay up there for three nights."

She looked at her empty glass as if blaming it for her loose tongue, then added, "Please don't mention it to

him. I really don't want to get involved and I shouldn't
have said anything."

Birch saw a wary spark in her eyes. He decided to
pursue his interest despite her hesitancy.

"Where does Pierce come from?"

Meg was repacking the basket. "He told me a couple
of months ago that he came here from Oklahoma." She
laughed. "He's told different stories to others. I guess it
depends on his mood. He told Doc Stanford that he'd
come from San Francisco of late and someone else was
told that Pierce came out of Illinois. It's not unusual for
people to come out here and lie about their origins. A
lot of us have something in our past that we want to
keep there."

Birch helped Meg back into the buggy, and they
started back for Grant's Pass. The sun was still shining,
but it was low in the sky, throwing shadows on the
granite rocks that lined the small dirt road. Birch noticed that the horse, Devil, was unusually skittish as they
approached Dead Indian Pass.

Just as they turned onto the shortcut, a gunshot
sounded from the hills above. Devil stopped and backed
up nervously a few paces. Before Birch could take better
hold of the reins to bring Devil back up to pace, another
shot rang out and Devil bolted forward.

Birch felt his head snap back. He lost his balance for
a moment, then looked at Meg. Her face was pale and
drawn. He felt her hand clutch his left arm as they
rounded a corner on two buggy wheels, tense springs
jouncing them around. Meg was thrown against Birch
as they came out of the bend, Devil's pounding hooves
beating out a frightening rhythm.

With the buggy swaying from side to side, Birch
grabbed a sidegrip firmly with his right hand and got

his bearings. The reins were loose and rested tenuously on the trappings. Birch knew that he would have to get hold of them in order to gain control of Devil again. He only hoped the slender trappings would hold his weight.

He climbed over the front of the buggy and put a tentative foot down on the right bar that extended along the length of the animal. As he put more weight on it, he slipped and grabbed the front of the buggy before trying again.

Birch tried to get a foothold again, this time successfully shifting his weight onto the bar. He grabbed the reins and straddled the bars, propping himself against the front of the buggy. His body caught the wind like a sail as he slowly reined Devil in. The jolting slowed and soon the horse and buggy were at a standstill. Devil continued to breath heavily from exertion.

"Are you okay?" Birch asked Meg.

Some color was coming back to her cheeks and she breathed a sigh of relief.

Then she laughed and said, "I should be asking you that. You're the one who risked his neck on the straddle bars."

Birch dusted himself off and made sure that Devil was calmed down enough before continuing the trip back to Grant's Pass. The buggy seemed to be intact as well. He realized that they had been very lucky. While they probably wouldn't have been killed by the runaway horse and buggy, they could have been seriously injured. Birch's naturally suspicious nature caused him to wonder if those gunshots had been fired specifically for his benefit.

Meg voiced his next thoughts. "Shouldn't we go back and find the person who fired those shots, Birch?"

He sighed. He really didn't want to think the worst

yet. He attempted to brush it off so as not to alarm her. "You're probably right, but by now he's long gone. Besides, I don't want you to get mixed up in this. We'd better head back to town."

But Meg was sharper than he'd given her credit for being.

"Birch?" Meg placed a hand on his forearm. "You're not going to do anything foolish, are you?"

"Well now, that depends on what you think is foolish, Meg."

"I heard that you were going to the mining camp this evening." Before he could ask who told her, she said, "Felix Pierce told me. When Luke Stone drinks, he can't keep his mouth shut, even when it's for his own good."

Birch's smile was grim. "I guess news travels fast around here. Does my visit to the camp pose a problem for some people in town?"

Meg's silence gave him his answer.

She continued to be unresponsive for a good part of the journey back to town, then suddenly said, "Look, I just want you to be a bit more careful. You may think those gunshots back there were just an accident, but I think that someone's trying to scare you into quitting this investigation. If you continue, you might get hurt."

"I appreciate your concern, Meg, but it's part of my job." Birch shook his head. "I didn't come here to make friends. I haven't exactly kept it a secret as to why I'm here."

"But what good will it do for you to talk to those miners?" In the fading sun, she looked like a young girl to Birch.

"I might be able to find out a thing or two from them. Someone might have seen or heard something that didn't seem significant at the time, but if I jog their memories, I might come up with a clue. They also need to be organized as a group if they want to make safe passage to Jacksonville until the thieves are caught."

Birch stopped there, realizing that he may have said too much. He still wasn't sure how far to trust Meg, and he realized that she had gotten far more information out of him than he had meant to give.

He cursed himself for being a fool about this woman. She could turn around and give that information to Pierce. On the other hand, he trusted his instincts, which told him that Meg wasn't the kind of woman who would betray him. He shook off these arguments uneasily as the buggy approached town.

Meg turned to him once more just before they reached town.

She spoke in a low voice as if the trees and boulders had ears. "Just be careful, Birch. Watch your back."

CHAPTER 8

AFTER Meg alighted from the buggy at the door of her saloon, Birch brought it back to the stable. When he descended from the carriage, he found Carver casually resting his foot on one of the wheels.

"Looks like you got yourself a little girlfriend, Birch."

Birch said sharply, "I thought Stubbs told you to stay away from me, Carver."

The deputy sneered and said, "I understand Dead Indian Pass can be kind of dangerous in a horse and buggy when someone's hunting up in the hills."

"What do you mean by that, Carver?" Birch asked casually, but his instincts told him to tread carefully. "Are you trying to tell me something?"

Carver looked contemptuously at Birch. "What would I want to tell you?"

Birch took a step toward Carver, intending to intimidate him. It seemed to be working. "Were you the one who scared the horse at Dead Indian Pass this afternoon?"

"Are you accusing me?" Carver looked slyly at Birch. His words came out carefully measured for effect. "I don't think I like your tone, Birch. Maybe we should settle this once and for all. Let's step outside."

There was something slightly ridiculous about the situation and Birch had to stifle an urge to laugh. It must have shown because a fleeting look of uncertainty

registered on the deputy's face before his resolve
returned.

"I'm the fastest gun in this town," he bragged. "I'm
not afraid to use my Colts. Step out in the street. I want
to kill you in front of witnesses."

Birch laughed at the youngster's dime-novel bluster.
He shook his head. "I don't think so."

Carver reached out and swung wildly at Birch's face.
Birch easily avoided the blow by stepping to the side and
grabbed Carver by the scruff of his neck and the back
of his jeans. He hoisted the troublesome deputy into a
convenient pile of hay, toppling his balance and his
dignity. With another swift gesture, Birch unholstered
Carver's guns and checked their chambers. Two bullets
were missing from one gun.

Birch emptied the guns and tossed them back to the
deputy.

He pushed his hat brim off his forehead and said,
"Well, I think we know who fired those shots out there
this afternoon, don't we, Carver?" Birch suddenly felt
tired. "Ever since I've been in Grant's Pass, you've made
it clear that you don't want me nosing around. Now if
you've got something to do with these road withdrawals,
you couldn't have been more obvious if you'd hung a
sign around your neck."

Birch turned to leave, then hesitated and added, "I'm
not interested in fighting you because I know who would
win."

Carver called after Birch, "I'll get you, Birch. You'll
pay for this."

Birch kept on walking.

Birch's ride out of town was uneventful. The sun had
set an hour before and a full moon was slowly creeping

up over the river. He turned to the right instead of taking the pass through to the river. Even without the full moon as his constant companion, Birch would have been able to make his way along the path by the sound of the Rogue River babbling along to his right.

But despite all the peace and quiet around him, he still felt uneasy, as if someone or something were watching him and biding time. He thought back to his last confrontation with Carver and tried to shake away the suspicious feeling he had for that deputy. Besides, Birch thought, I have other things on my mind that are far more important than an eighteen-year-old with an itchy trigger finger and a deputy's badge.

Before long, he came to a crest in the path that led down and wound around toward the sound of voices, music, and the glow of campfires. He dismounted and led his horse, Cactus, into the site, knowing full well that a stranger on horseback was more likely to be shot first and asked questions later.

A large-boned woman was tending a large pot on a fire. She looked up at him with dull eyes, then called for Stone. From one of the myriad tents propped on the hard, unyielding ground, a flap opened up and Luke Stone emerged. He caught sight of Birch and greeted him.

"Didn't think you'd make it tonight. Heard you'd been shot at this afternoon." Stone grinned.

Birch secured the reins to a nearby branch and replied, "Word certainly gets around quick here in Grant's Pass. It was only a few hours ago. I just returned the horse and buggy before heading out this way."

Stone nodded once slowly. "One of the miners heard the gunshots this afternoon. He was hunting for tonight's meal and wanted to find out who was shooting nearby. He caught sight of your runaway buggy on the path below and recognized you."

"Did he get a look at the person who fired the shots?"

Stone shook his head. "No, but later he saw someone riding in the other direction. Looked somewhat like that young redheaded deputy."

"Carver?" Birch was not surprised, but he felt obliged to ask.

Stone shrugged. "He heard the sound of a horse at full gallop on the other side of the hill, but he was too late to get anything more than a glimpse of the rider. But he definitely had red hair. The shots were fired from a six-shooter, not a rifle. And I think you know that no one goes hunting with a revolver."

Birch asked, "Will I be able to speak to all the miners here tonight?"

"Most of the miners around here have joined this camp and share chores," Stone explained. "I've talked to the few who live outside the camp and most of them will be here tonight if they have anything to tell you. We have over fifty men here in this campsite and about seven or eight who live along the other side of the river."

Birch followed Stone around the camp as Stone explained the camp setup with sweeping gestures.

"I came out here with my family three years ago when I heard about the gold. We're originally from Kansas, but our farm hadn't been doing so well. There'd been a drought that killed most of our crops. Our neighbors didn't fare so well, either.

"Since I was a preacher as well as a farmer, I decided to take my family west and lay claim to some of the land. I spoke God's word along the way for money to feed my family. By the time we settled here and filed a claim, I'd also saved enough for us to live on for a few months."

Two boys, aged about fourteen and twelve, came up to the reverend. He put his hands on the boys' shoulders. "These are my sons, Jedediah and Moses. They help their pa pan for gold."

Birch addressed the eldest, a sullen thin boy with a sallow complexion. "Nice to meet you, son. How's your claim doing? Do you find much dust for your pa?"

The boy shrank close to his father and looked away. It was the younger one, a smaller, rosy-cheeked lad, who spoke up. "We ain't supposed to boast about our good fortune. Pa says it's a sin." The boy turned his bright eyes on Birch. "You're the man who's gonna get those road robbers, ain't you?"

Stone laughed and sent them on their way. "They're miners through and through. I told them it's a sin to boast about our claim so no one could try to give us trouble or try panning our claim. Miners are a suspicious lot, especially when they've struck a vein. If you go around bragging about your motherlode, you might wind up with a bullet in your back one night."

"If you're all so suspicious of each other," Birch said, "then why do you all live in such close quarters?"

Stone laughed again. "Why, that's an easy one to answer, Birch. It's easier to keep an eye on each other." He changed the subject. "You're not from around here, are you?"

"Texas was my home." Birch looked up into the trees surrounding the camp.

"What'd you do there?"

"I rode with the Rangers."

Stone nodded his approval. "That there's a real tough outfit. You must be pretty good with a gun and a horse. How come you're out here now?"

Birch had his answer ready. "I needed a change."

Stone had stepped outside a tent. "Hey Dewey!"

After a moment of shuffling and clattering, a hulking figure crept out. He stood six feet tall, had bushy black hair, and a pasty moon-shaped face. "Evening, Lucas."

The reverend turned to Birch and said, "Dewey's the only one who'll call me by my formal first name. Can't break him of the habit. He calls everyone by their first names." He turned to Dewey again. "This here's Birch, ah, I don't know his first name . . ."

Birch supplied it. "Jefferson Birch."

Stone continued, "Yeah. He's here on behalf of the county sheriff to look into the robberies and deaths of some of the miners around here."

Dewey was silent for a minute, sizing up Birch. Birch did likewise, taking in the book held by the giant. Dewey could read, a sign of an educated man.

"Well, Jefferson, how may I help you?"

Birch smiled at the soft-spoken man. "Have you been to Jacksonville since the ambushes began?"

Dewey shook his head. "I haven't had a strike since the end of last year. I don't go to Jacksonville unless I hit a vein. Most miners don't want to keep nuggets around their stake for too long. Too many thieves around here."

Birch turned to Luke Stone. "Why did those miners go to Jacksonville alone? You should be organizing yourselves by going in large groups instead of taking your chances separately."

The two miners looked at each other with amusement. Stone said, "Why that's a good idea, Mr. Birch." He turned to Dewey. "Why don't we round up a few of the miners and Mr. Birch can explain it to them."

Birch detected sarcasm in the reverend's tone, but brushed it off. "I know that the men are suspicious of one another, but in times like this, you should pull together. It would only be a temporary measure."

Birch sensed that the amusement had passed. Stone was serious when he replied, "Maybe you can talk some sense into them."

They moved off into the darkness to gather the meeting, pausing at various tents to spread the word. Birch moved on to the next row, where the musicians were still playing. Men began to straggle into the clearing and gradually, the music stopped as the buzz of conversation became louder. Many of the miners cradled a bottle of rye or whiskey. Most of them looked tired and grubby after a day of stooping in the riverbed or, for the luckier ones, mining a vein.

Stone stood near the fire and looked around at the miners. They looked back at him expectantly. Some miners looked curiously at Birch, who sat off to Stone's left.

"Friends," Stone addressed them in his best preaching voice, "we have a visitor in our midst tonight who is asking questions about the spate of robberies and killings. Several miners here tonight have been held up on the Jacksonville road and are here to tell about it. If you have any information—you may have seen something that didn't seem important at the time—talk to Birch about it."

Stone hadn't bothered to introduce Birch, he just indicated where the ex-Ranger was. Birch figured that most of the miners knew who he was and why he was here.

The miners glared at each other suspiciously. Birch began to think that no one would step forward.

Stone turned to a man with a lantern jaw. "Jawbone, you went to Jacksonville about two months ago."

Jawbone smiled ruefully and rubbed his massive chin. "Well, I was going to. I started out the day after I'd mined a good vein on my claim. Barely an hour later, these outlaws jumped me and took all my gold."

Birch asked, "Did you recognize any of them?"

The miner shook his head sadly. "They were all wearing bandannas. I couldn't tell how tall they were because they were all on horses—except the man who picked up my gold when I threw it down. He was tall and skinny."

"Did you see what color his hair was?"

Jawbone thought a moment. He shook his head again. "It could have been brown or red. It wasn't blond or black hair, that's for sure."

Birch asked, "Had you told anyone that you were going to Jacksonville? Did anyone know that you'd hit a motherlode?"

Jawbone looked offended. "Of course not. I wouldn't tell anyone."

Dewey added, "The first time we heard of Jawbone's trip was after he'd been robbed."

Stone said, "But that don't mean that someone who wanted to find out couldn't have done so. He has to ride through town and there's no way around these mountains. If a horse broke a leg in the mountains, a man could be stranded."

"And the only reason a miner would ride through town would be if he was on his way to Jacksonville," Birch concluded. "From my own experience, news travels fast around here even if you haven't talked to anyone."

A buzz of agreement rose up from the miners. Birch felt that with all this camaraderie, now was a good time to bring up the idea of working together.

He stood up and called for their attention. "Before I leave here tonight, I'd like to ask you to form some sort of organized protection for yourselves when you go to Jacksonville. I understand there's a lot of petty disagreements and suspicion among you. I hope you'll put it all aside until I catch the outlaws."

One miner stood up, a small wiry man with a set of scruffy whiskers and a shapeless hat. "I'm with you, Birch. As long as I don't have to ride with the Ridley brothers."

"Why not?"

The miner squinted in the light of the campfire. "Because those no-good snakes jumped Elijah Stearns's claim once he was dead. Didn't give us a fair chance at it."

Stone spoke up. "Now, Jake. You know that was all done legal-like."

"I don't care. I don't want them getting any protection from me."

Another miner jumped up. "And I don't think Old Man Caruthers should be in on this either. He's been panning on my claim when I'm not there. I caught him once. Claimed he'd lost his bifocals and it was hard for him to tell one part of the river from the other. I won't be in on this if he is."

A voice from the shadows spoke. "Oh yeah? Well, I ain't been panning in your measly riverbed, Gimpy." The glint of a knife shone in the firelight. "And I'll fight you for calling me a liar and a cheat."

"Just telling the truth," the other miner muttered.

As the two adversaries circled each other in an open space, Birch and Stone tried to reason with the rest of the miners, but more exceptions to the protection rule kept cropping up. The shouting escalated and more fights began.

Finally Stone drew Birch aside. "I don't think we're going to get through to them tonight. But I'll keep working on it. When you organize, you have to protect all or none."

Birch shook his head in amazement. "They sure hold a lot of grudges. I hope you can talk some sense into them."

"Like I said before, miners are a suspicious lot, all right. That's why it's called gold *fever*. It makes them crazy."

"So how come," Birch asked, "you're not out there fighting, too?"

Stone looked over at his tent. "I got my family with me. Most of those men left their families behind or they marry after they start mining for gold." He sighed heavily. "The gold fever's already set in by then and even the love of a woman won't change a man who's already rounded the bend. I've seen it happen time and time again. But I've got my family and my preaching."

Gunfire exploded from the direction of the camp. Stone didn't seem fazed by it at all. "That's just to put a scare in someone. Probably Caruthers trying to scare some sense into Gimpy."

Birch touched his gunbelt. He took his guns seriously, never drawing them unless he was provoked. After a few more words with Stone, Birch rode out of the camp.

CHAPTER 9

IT was deathly quiet on the road back. The moon hung full and bright over the river. Birch heard an owl's hooting and Cactus's hooves striking the packed dirt of the path. A rustle of leaves, as some nocturnal animal hunted for its meal, reminded Birch that he hadn't had supper yet. The rhythmic creaking of his well-worn saddle beneath him lulled Birch into a groggy state, something he had promised himself wouldn't happen.

A burst of gunfire scared Birch's horse. Cactus whinnied nervously and skittered sideways. Birch lost his balance and struck the ground hard on his right side. When he recovered, he felt something warm and sticky running down his left arm. A bullet had creased the flesh just below his shoulder. Birch winced when he touched the injury, but determined that it was a clean wound and was bleeding freely. But his left arm was practically useless. He took hold of Cactus's reins and led the animal toward a ravine nearby. Making sure that they were partially hidden by bushes and rocks, he secured the reins to a tree, then crept along the ravine until he'd almost reached a large rock. With his right hand, he unholstered his gun.

Another shot rang out and Birch dove for a boulder. He looked out into the moonlit night and tried to determine where the shots were coming from. Silence. Cursing the quiet landscape, he aimed a wild shot in hopes of drawing fire. Birch was rewarded with a volley of returned gunfire, but he still couldn't see where the ambusher was shooting from. At least he'd narrowed it down to some bushes and trees near the river on the other side of the road.

His arm was hurting like hell now. He pulled a bandanna out of his pocket, wound it tightly around his arm, and secured it. The pain made Birch even more determined to find his hidden enemy. This was no coincidence, he thought. Someone had followed him out of town at a leisurely distance, then waited for him to head back to Grant's Pass. It seemed as though the whole town knew he was going to the mining camp tonight, so he couldn't narrow it down. Birch wondered if Carver was the one shooting at him. It wouldn't surprise him.

Birch gauged the distance between his place behind the boulder and the unknown gunman. It was a good fifty feet away, if not more, and if he stood up, the moonlight would show his outline clear enough for even an amateur marksman to finish the job. And whoever was out there was a good shot. The bullet wound in Birch's upper left arm was a sign that the enemy wanted a gunfight, not just to shoot Birch down in cold blood. Revenge meant that Carver had to be behind this.

The ambusher had the advantage of knowing exactly where Birch was. Without knowing where his foe was hiding, Birch couldn't get off a clean shot, even in the moonlight. He looked up at the moon with its big white face shining so brightly on the Rogue. And what he saw drifting across the sky toward the moon was almost too good to be true: a cloud floated lazily nearby and would soon obscure the clean white landscape below.

Birch readied himself. With his one good arm, he pulled off his boots, silently cursing the shooter for ruining the use of one arm. He promised himself that if it was Jim Carver out there, he'd return the favor. He'd met men like Carver before. They were so eager to bully people that they never spent much time growing up. Anxious to hang scalps on their belts, they only felt good when they were able to boast about how many men they had killed. As far as Birch was concerned, Carver was a dead man already—he just didn't know it yet.

Just before the cloud covered the moon, Birch fired another round and in return heard the ping of the gunman's bullets on the boulder that sheltered him. It was getting too close. A moment later, Birch rolled out from behind the rock and crept, bootless, along the ravine. When he got far enough away from the source of the shots, he scrambled out of the ravine and crossed the road. The ground on the river's side was unpleasantly soft and damp and his socks soon became encrusted with mud, but it muffled the sound of his approach.

Birch kept his gun at the ready. His arm still throbbed, but it was now a dull pain that he could almost ignore. Behind a tree about thirty feet away, Birch caught sight of the gunman. His attention was still on the spot where Birch had been earlier. He came up behind the lanky figure and grabbed him around the neck with his good arm.

"What's the matter, Carver?" Birch asked in a dry tone. "You missed shooting me in the back. This is your idea of a fair fight? Drop your rifle."

Carver made a strangled sound and dropped his rifle. "You son of a bitch."

The loss of blood made Birch feel queasy. His grip on Carver loosened as he started to take a deep breath. Instead, he felt the deputy's bootheel kick him sharply in the ankle. Then he dug an elbow into Birch's ribs. Birch tasted dirt and tried to shake off that dazed feeling he always got when he was shot. Somehow, he managed to stagger to his feet and grab Carver before he reached his rifle.

"No," was all Birch got out before Carver twisted around and hit him in the face. He must have released his grip on the deputy because the next thing he knew, Carver was diving for his fallen rifle. Birch grabbed him by the shirt and pulled him up short, hauling off a right to the deputy's jaw. Birch watched as Carver tried to shake off the punch. The deputy brought his hand up as if to touch his slightly swelled jaw, but instead, he punched Birch in his wounded shoulder, knocking him off balance and on his ass. He looked up at Carver, who hovered above him wearing an expression that seemed to be mad with glee at Birch's suffering. Carver turned to grab his rifle. Birch grimaced and reached for his Colt.

"This will show you that I'm better than you, Birch," Carver was saying as Birch got a shot off. The deputy's left leg crumpled underneath him. He looked in shock at the blood and shattered bone.

Birch said, "It's over, Carver."

The deputy grimaced, then said, "I'm still faster than you, Birch." And he swung his rifle to shoot.

But the shot went wild because Birch shot Carver first. The deputy looked at his gut wound in surprise. His mouth opened and he clutched his middle, hoping to stop his life blood from seeping out. He looked at Birch as if he couldn't quite comprehend what had just happened to him.

Birch lowered his gun, regretting the action he'd had to take. "You might have been faster with a six-gun,

Carver, but a rifle is a whole different story." His face softened a little as he looked into the young man's dying face. "Son, did you have anything to do with those road withdrawals? Is there anything you want to tell me before you die?"

Birch could see Carver's mouth working, but the sound was so soft that he had to bend down a little to hear.

Carver said, "Yes, I was in on it."

"Can you tell me who else is involved? I know you couldn't have pulled them off by yourself." Carver beckoned Birch to come closer. He was getting weaker.

"I'll never tell you, you son of a bitch."

He weakly spat in Birch's face, then laid back and died.

The marshal's house was on the edge of town. Stubbs came to the door with a look of annoyance on his face. "What is it, Birch? Can't it wait till morning? You must know what time it is!"

Birch shook his head. "Nope. It can't wait. I just killed a man outside of town in self-defense. You knew him."

"Well, don't beat around the bush. Tell me his name, damn it!"

"Jim Carver." Birch gestured toward the two horses tethered outside on Stubbs's fence.

Henry Stubbs squinted at the animals. "What is this, Birch, some kind of a joke? Jim is supposed to be at the office on duty. This town doesn't run by itself. In fact, right now he should be making rounds to all the saloons to make sure no fights have broken out."

"I guess the deputy thought the town could take care of itself while he went after me with a rifle." Birch winced as he indicated his left arm. "Where was Carver this afternoon?"

"Why?"

"Someone scared my horse with gunshots. Could that have been your deputy?"

Stubbs's expression hardened. "My deputy was in town earlier today. Miners hunt for food out where you were heading. You have no call to accuse . . ."

They were interrupted by Felix Pierce. "Good evening, gentlemen. It's a little late in the evening for business, isn't it?" He dismounted and tied his horse's reins loosely to a hitching post outside the marshal's house, pausing for a moment to look at the body draped over Carver's horse.

Stubbs replied, "I might ask you the same thing, Pierce."

"I run a saloon, which has just closed, in case you've forgotten, Marshal. I'm on my way home." Pierce indicated the two horses nearby. "Looks like you've had some trouble. Is anyone going to do something about that dead body?"

Stubbs grunted and detached himself from his doorway to examine the body. "That body, Felix, was my deputy. Mr. Birch here killed him. I have a good mind to throw him in jail."

The marshal wasn't being very rational at the moment. Birch figured that being awakened from a sound sleep with news of a killing could unhinge almost anyone. But he thought it best to set the record straight.

Birch turned to Stubbs. "You forgot to mention that it was in self-defense, Marshal."

Pierce listened impassively, then addressed Stubbs. "Birch has a point, Marshal. Jim Carver threatened

Birch this morning at my saloon in front of at least a
dozen witnesses."

Stubbs peered at Birch and Pierce, then said in a
peeved voice, "I know, I know. That boy wasn't worth
his pay, but he was my sister's boy." He got a worried
look on his face. "Guess someone had better get the
doctor."

Pierce said curtly, "I'll go. It's on my way home." He
got back on his horse and rode out.

Birch asked, "Do you want me to stay and answer
questions?"

Stubbs shook his head wearily. "Unless you want the
doc to take a look at that arm, you can go on back to
your room and get some sleep. I overreacted earlier.
Guess I'm just tired, son. Sorry about that." Birch indicated that it was okay, then Stubbs added, "When he
wanted to do something, he never listened to anyone,
least of all me. And when he took a dislike to someone"—Stubbs looked sharply at Birch—"he didn't
change his mind. He liked to kill, that's for sure. Always
was proud of being the fastest gun in town. For what
that was worth. I kept telling him that someday someone
would come along who was faster. But he liked to bully
people."

"Why did you make him deputy?" Birch wanted to
know.

Stubbs shook his head. "I thought it would keep him
out of trouble if he worked on the side of the law."

Birch went back to the hotel. His arm had stopped
hurting and he figured that the doctor would have his
hands full tonight. He'd barely taken his boots off
before he was asleep.

CHAPTER 10

AFTER breakfast the next morning, Birch went down to the stables to free Cactus from his stall. He rode up to Stubbs's office to find out who was going to replace Carver as deputy.

Stubbs looked up briefly when Birch entered the tiny room. "Morning, Marshal."

Henry Stubbs grunted and leaned back in his chair. "What do you want, Birch? You got another body for me?"

Birch shook his head impatiently at Stubbs's unnecessary sarcasm. "I just stopped by to see how you were getting along without a deputy. Do you need a replacement?"

"Nope, not yet."

"It shouldn't be too hard to fill Carver's boots, I'd think. You run a clean town."

Stubbs's laugh was dry. "It was a clean town until you came along, son."

Birch ignored the caustic remark. "I've been a Texas Ranger, so if you need to deputize me temporarily, I will oblige. I feel some responsibility for what happened last night, but I didn't force a rifle into Carver's hand."

Stubbs nodded. "I appreciate the offer. I'll keep that in mind. Where are you headed today?"

"Don't know yet. I'll keep you informed."

Stubbs took out a cheroot and bit off the end. "Loggers' payroll's coming in a day or so from now. I could find out exactly when it comes in for you." He lit the cigar and sucked in the thick slow smoke.

"Might not be a bad idea. I'll be back later."

The road to the logging camp took a sharp right on the way to the Rogue River. The road was all uphill, winding through the pines. It was wider than the main road because it was a skid road to roll the cut logs down. A man ascending a skid road had to keep his eyes and ears open for the sound of a rolling log. An experienced logger might be able to escape a runaway log, but someone not familiar with logging camps might not be so lucky.

A stillness hung in the air, becoming more hushed as Birch and Cactus traveled further uphill. The air became sharper, stinging his lungs if he inhaled too deeply. It invigorated him.

Soon the path evened out and Birch began to see men hollering to each other and to hear the sound of bandsaws scraping wood, eating away at the trunks of tall tan oaks.

A large clearing loomed up ahead with dun-colored tents scattered here and there. The camp was almost empty, with the exception of the cook and one or two men. A short, stout man, obviously in charge, walked purposefully toward Birch. From his carriage, Birch guessed that this was the logging camp manager.

"Mr. Birch, I presume." The German accent was thick. "My name is Gustav Bierbohm. Swede told me you would be visiting my camp."

They shook hands.

A tinny clang sounded from one of the tents. Bierbohm said, "Supper. Have you eaten?"

Birch shook his head and followed Bierbohm to the

tent. They bypassed the line of hungry, eager men—it was one of the few privileges the manager had in a logging camp. Birch received a plateful of mashed potatoes with chunks of meat floating in a brown gravy. A mug of beer was thrust into his free hand as he came to the end of the supper line, and he followed Bierbohm to a corner table.

Birch caught sight of Swede heading toward the table with four other loggers. Bierbohm explained, "Swede has organized my most loyal men to be at your disposal. You are in charge."

"Why haven't you varied the delivery of your payroll to confuse the outlaws?" asked Birch.

"I tried that," Bierbohm replied, "but it didn't work."

"We think they have a lookout," Swede explained, "at the beginning of the run."

Birch nodded. It wasn't uncommon for an organized gang to have one member ride into a town and watch the stagecoach being loaded up, then pass along information to the leader in plenty of time to set up an ambush. It wasn't as profitable to hold up a stagecoach without a payroll. Passengers generally didn't carry much cash with them.

The German shrugged philosophically. "It's no big secret that the payroll is delivered on the fifth of every month. There are so many people who have contact with the payroll."

"How does the payroll reach the camp? Do you pick it up?"

Bierbohm shook his head. "My son waits for the stagecoach in Grant's Pass, then brings it here."

"And he's never been ambushed?"

"No. The marshal keeps the town clean. And my son can take care of himself." Bierbohm indicated a beefy red-faced man with hands twice as large as an average man's. He was in the middle of a beer-chugging contest with another giant. Birch wondered why Bierbohm's son wasn't here with his father. After all, it was a family business. Maybe the family business extended as far as robbing miners and the logging payroll.

"Tell me, Bierbohm," Birch asked, "is there any reason you should suspect anyone in your camp?"

The German looked puzzled. "Suspect them of what?"

"Supplying information to outlaws and sharing in the money that's stolen."

Bierbohm sputtered, "That's ridiculous!"

"Just thought I'd ask," Birch shrugged. "It's part of my job."

"It just took me by surprise," Bierbohm answered. "I hope you're not serious. If the stealing continues, this logging operation will end and all of us will be out of jobs."

Bierbohm cleared his throat and, as if nothing happened, said, "Now then, as I have said before, my son and several others have volunteered to aid you. All you need to do is ask. My son, Wolfgang, is a very strong man and can be very handy if you're on the wrong end of a fight." He turned back to business. "Now, Mr. Birch, what do you require?"

"What do you want me to do exactly?"

Bierbohm leaned forward. "I want this payroll. I am willing to pay for it. As I've said before, if I don't get it, we are out of business. I want it to travel safely through to Grant's Pass. If you are successful, I will pay you well."

"I can do that with some help from your men." Birch

turned to Swede and the rest. "I need volunteers to ride shotgun with me."

Bierbohm warned him, "All of my men are loggers, Mr. Birch. Not hired guns. None of them would have the slightest idea of what to do if they were ambushed."

"I'm not looking to get anyone killed. I just want two or three men who can handle a gun." Birch looked around the table, then added, "I can't say there isn't some risk involved, but if you can keep a cool head, I could use the help."

Swede spoke up. "I haven't handled a gun for a long time, but I will go."

Birch knew that this was a big risk for Swede. He had a wife back in Norway to consider. It was one thing risking his neck in a logging camp—he knew the dangers. But riding shotgun could be very unhealthy if they were ambushed and the outlaws got a little trigger-happy. A look of understanding passed between Birch and Swede.

On the heels of Swede's offer came another volunteer. "I have hunted game around here sometimes with a rifle. I'm not used to a pistol, but if you just want a body, I'm your man." This came from a husky dark man who spoke in a halting foreign accent. Birch guessed that he was French.

Another voice boomed over the din, thick and slow with a gutteral German accent. "I will accompany these men as well. I can't handle a gun very well, either, but I think my size will make up for it."

Birch turned around to face Bierbohm's son, Wolfgang. Gustav nodded his approval. Birch caught the same uncertain look on the Swede's face that he felt. While Wolfgang was even larger than the Swede, size wouldn't stop bullets. But it seemed to be settled for the father—his son would accompany them. Bierbohm couldn't spare another man; the logs were all being sent down the chute and rolled down the river to the storage area tomorrow.

It was agreed that Swede, Wolfgang, and the Frenchman (whose nickname was Duke) would meet Birch outside of Grant's Pass the next morning and they would ride to Jacksonville together. The loggers might think that Birch was being too cautious about meeting them outside of town, but Birch didn't want to take any chances. If they met in Grant's Pass, they were open to scrutiny, and if there was someone in town who was connected to the gang responsible for the road withdrawals, they could be ambushed on the way to Jacksonville instead.

Birch was eating breakfast at Meg's saloon the next morning when the marshal stopped by for coffee. Stubbs swaggered over to Birch's table and said, "I saw you riding up to the logging camp yesterday, Birch."

Birch looked at Stubbs over his bacon and eggs. He reached for his coffee mug. "I might have been going to the mining camp or maybe just scouting the area."

Stubbs said easily, "You've already been to the mining camp, and if you were scouting the area, you'd want to go out on the Jacksonville road, not toward the river."

Birch nodded.

Stubbs said, "Did you learn anything useful?"

Birch didn't feel like being reasonable so early in the morning. He said, "Why don't you ride up there and ask Bierbohm yourself?"

Stubbs laughed.

Birch got up and paid for his meal. The marshal silently followed Birch out of the saloon.

"Heading somewhere, Birch?"

Birch was getting tired of Stubbs's dogged determination to learn something. He turned around and faced the marshal with a hard look. "You told me to come to you with any information I might gather. Well, I don't know anything yet. When I do, I'll let you know."

Stubbs looked surprised and a little hurt. "I'm just worried about you, son. Ever since my deputy tried to kill you, I'm trying to keep a closer eye on you. Someone else may want to try it and I'm just watching your back."

Birch let out a long sigh as he adjusted the cinch strap on Cactus's saddle. "I appreciate your concern, Marshal. But I can watch my own back."

Henry Stubbs's tone grew defensive. "What you mean is you don't trust no one. Not even the town marshal. I guess you figure anyone could be the lookout for that so-called organized outlaw gang that Sheriff Calhoun told you about."

Birch cut him off. "I can't rule out any possibilities, Marshal. The sheriff has his reasons for suspecting these road withdrawals are the work of an organized gang. As for suspecting you, I can't say one way or another. Now if you don't mind, I'll be on my way."

With that, Birch mounted Cactus and rode out of town.

The three loggers were already waiting for him. It took them most of the morning, pacing their horses at a brisk trot whenever possible. They didn't want to wind the horses, but they needed to be in Jacksonville by early afternoon, in time to accompany the stage back to Grant's Pass.

At several points along the road, Birch slowed down, scanning the landscape on both sides of the path. One time, he muttered, "This is a likely place for a road withdrawal," within Swede's hearing range, but other than that, he was silent.

They reached Jacksonville in time for a midday meal at a saloon across the road from the telegraph office. The stagecoach rested in front, empty and silent. Birch noted that there were no passengers pacing back and forth near the stage, waiting to get to Grant's Pass.

Birch told Swede and the others that he would join up with them at the saloon after taking care of some business, then disappeared in the direction of the telegraph office up the street. Within half an hour, he returned and ate his meal while keeping an eye out for any loiterers outside near the stagecoach.

Since the Jacksonville telegraph office was a central meeting place for many people, it was hard to focus on one man in particular who looked suspicious. Most of the men who lingered there had a shifty look about them. At one point, Birch caught sight of a man who casually walked over to a reined horse, mounted, and directed his horse out of town—toward Grant's Pass!

Before they paid for their meals and headed back to their horses, Birch addressed all of them. "I just want to remind you that riding shotgun involves some risk. I don't want any of you taking foolish chances if we get ambushed. Just let them take the strongbox. Your lives are more important than the money."

Duke shook his head. "I need that money to send back to my parents in France. I cannot afford to let it go."

Birch said, "You must trust me. Do not endanger your lives by trying to outdraw an outlaw with a gun already in his hand. The money will get through. But if we are ambushed, let them take the strongbox."

Swede and Wolfgang nodded, Duke following reluctantly. He looked troubled and intense after the talk.
Birch would have to keep a close eye on Duke. It was too
late to send the Frenchman back to the camp.

The stagedriver went by the name of Garrity. He
didn't seem to have a first name, or if he did, he'd long
ago forgotten it. Garrity was thin and wiry with long
hair carelessly caught in back with an old rawhide boot-
lace. When he smiled, he displayed a splendid set of
gums with a few teeth added for decoration.

Garrity was quite talkative during the first part of the
trip. "You boys from around here?"

Birch answered. "Nope."

"Me either," Garrity went on. "I'm from back east
near Ohio. Came out here just before the gold rush of
forty-nine and haven't been back since. Shame about
them gold miners out near Grant's Pass, getting waylaid
like that. Last one was kilt. But I guess that's why I never
cottoned much to mining for gold. I'd rather earn my
money at a regular job, take the gold miners' money the
easy way. Too many people want that gold."

Birch said, "I guess you've never been ambushed
while driving this stagecoach, then."

"Yep, I was. Didn't say I didn't mind a little risk. Just
don't like going around wearing a great big sign saying,
'Shoot me. I have a big bag of gold in my saddlebags.'
Think it's damn foolish."

Birch was about to ask the driver about his ambush,
but Garrity didn't need any prompting.

"Yep, I was on the second stage to be held up. Don't
want to be held up again soon. My wife wants me to quit
driving, but it's a good job and I like traveling this road.
Hope you fellas can hold them outlaws off if we get held
up this time."

Birch smiled and nodded. He exchanged an amused glance with Swede as Garrity continued to regale the four shotgun riders with his experiences as a stagecoach driver.

Birch listened with only half an ear as his eyes continued to scan the landscape up ahead, sometimes resting on an area particularly susceptible to ambushes. Swede and Wolfgang flanked the stagecoach while Duke rode to one side and Birch scouted on ahead. When he rode too far ahead, he'd stop and listen for the snort of a hidden horse or the rustle of leaves while he waited for the entourage to catch up.

The first three quarters of the journey went smoothly, but soon the road narrowed and ravines ran alongside. Birch stuck closer to the stagecoach now.

It was about five miles outside of Grant's Pass that the road agents emerged and surrounded them. "Throw down the strongbox and be damned quick about it!" were the first words heard.

Birch silently cursed himself, but he knew deep down that there was little he could have done to prevent it from happening. He'd counted on scaring the ambushers with the large number of shotgun riders surrounding the stagecoach. He also hoped that Wolfgang and Swede's size would make even the most determined outlaw think twice before holding up the stagecoach.

But it had backfired. These outlaws were bolder and cleverer than most of the yellow dogs that haunted the roadsides.

Birch glanced sideways at the leader, a narrow fellow whose face was hidden by a bandanna. He gauged the masked man's height at six feet, if he were standing instead of sitting on a horse. He caught the faint scent of sweet pomade in the air. Birch studied the leader's horse, hoping to find some distinguishing mark visible to his trained eye, but the horse was an unremarkable brown with a white mark near his forelock. It was a common enough distinction, as Birch had seen at least two horses boarded in the stables with the same mark. He would have to examine it more closely in order to make a confident identification.

Nevertheless, Birch had a strong suspicion that the leader was from Grant's Pass or Jacksonville. Most outlaws didn't bother to pomade their hair, and their hands weren't as clean and soft as the masked stranger's were.

Birch looked around at the other loggers. Swede and Duke were to his left in front and Wolfgang was in back of the coach to the right. Garrity was still sitting on the driver's perch.

The masked leader harshly addressed Wolfgang. "You in the back! Get up here." When the large German complied with a start, Birch heard guns cock, then the leader added, "Slowly. You don't want to die young."

Birch felt dread as he swung his gaze over to Duke. Anger, fright, and mad rage swept over Duke's face. Birch silently tried to catch the Frenchman's eye, but Duke's hand was already hovering over his holster.

Birch whispered hoarsely, "Duke, no!" At the same time, he heard a gun's report.

Duke sat frozen on his horse for a moment longer, then slid off his horse in slow motion. The spell broke when Birch heard Swede yelling and Duke's body landed with a thud on the ground.

Instinctively, Birch leapt from his horse, his hand reaching for his gun as he headed for the safety of the ravine. He crouched down and ran crablike along the deep bank.

More shots rang out. The leader had seen Birch's retreat and shouted to his companions. Birch did what any good former Ranger would have done in his situation—he reversed directions and went back to his former position.

They were expecting him to attack them from the ravine, so he crept out of it. With Garrity's help, who, by this time was flat on the stage roof, gave him a nod that told him not to hesitate and move fast, Birch darted across the road and flattened himself against the far side of the stagecoach.

The leader called out, "It's no use, Birch." Birch raised his eyebrows at the sound of his name. The outlaw knew him by sight, and that narrowed it down to Grant's Pass. "We've got you and your friends covered."

Birch lowered himself slightly and removed his hat. With his shoulder aligned against the corner of the carriage, he not only had a view of the outlaws, but could make out Swede's arm and the top of his head behind an outcropping of rock and the shooting end of Wolfgang's rifle behind a tree. Duke was not there.

Some of the gang members had dismounted, but two were still on their horses. All had their guns drawn, and those on the ground had taken cover across the road from where Swede and the German were sheltered. Swede caught Birch's eye and together they opened fire on the desperadoes. Wolfgang followed suit.

One man caught a bullet, spun around, and fell to the ground like a pile of sticks. The others scattered. The men on horseback escaped in a flurry of dust and hooves, heading toward Jacksonville.

Birch noticed that one of the escaped outlaws was the leader. The two men who were left returned wild fire as they grabbed horses and tried to mount the already skittish animals. Birch got off a few wild shots to scare them. Swede and Wolfgang followed his lead.

Both of the outlaws were half hiding behind their trotting horses. One man looked like he had his foot caught in the stirrup and couldn't get a leg up. The pounding hooves became fainter and fainter as they rounded the bend toward Jacksonville.

The silence that comes after a gun battle settled in. Birch inspected the road and ravine from his position, Garrity from his post, and when they'd agreed that it was clear, they moved out into the open. Duke's lifeless body lay on the ground. Swede and Wolfgang went directly to their friend. Birch inspected the unmoving figure of the unlucky outlaw.

Swede was checking Duke's eyes when Birch approached. Wolfgang looked up and shook his head.

Birch's jaw was set as he gazed down at Duke's lifeless body. He was angry at himself for not having kept a closer eye on the Frenchman. He should have talked to Duke before they rode into Jacksonville. He should have explained to all of them that the payroll was not in the strongbox. He should have trusted them more. He should have. Swede must have sensed the frustration Birch was feeling. He said to Birch, "Duke never was much good at taking orders. He wouldn't have listened to you, no matter what you said."

Birch picked up a stone and flung it far into the ravine. "There's something I kept quiet about because I thought the less people who knew about it, the less chance there would be that the information would slip to the ambushers." He faced them. "The payroll was transferred from the strongbox to my saddlebags. That's why I told you all not to challenge them if they

ambushed us." Birch shook his head. "If I'd told you . . ."
Wolfgang's face turned red, his neck bulging with
angry roped veins. His accent became very heavy when
he was angry. "If you'd told us, Duke would still be
alive." He took a step toward Birch. Birch wasn't looking
forward to taking on the boss's giant son. Before Wolfgang reached Birch, Swede stepped in.

"Wolfgang, you know as well as I do that Duke
wouldn't have paid attention. He wanted to fight those
outlaws for all the wrongs that have been done to us
over the past few months. He wanted to even the score.
He drew his gun on armed men back there. He did
exactly what Birch told him not to do."

The big German's face relaxed. He shook his head
sadly. "He was a good fighter. But you're right. He
didn't have any sense." Wolfgang looked at Birch and
clapped a large calloused hand on his shoulder. "I am
sorry, my friend. You were just looking out for the
company's interests."

Birch said, "I hate to see those interests paid for with
blood."

They loaded the body into the empty stagecoach and
headed back to Grant's Pass. As they rode along, Birch
thought about Duke's death.

"Maybe he figured it was better to die than to keep
fighting a losing battle," Birch thought. He realized that
those words rang true for himself.

He had a desire to be reunited with Audrey and his
baby son. Maybe taking this job was just a way of slowly
killing himself. He'd done everything but hang a sign
on himself, advertising that he wanted to die. Birch's
saving grace was his experience with the Texas Rangers.
His instinct for survival overrode his grief.

Lost in his thoughts, Birch realized that Swede and Wolfgang had just been talking about Duke. Then he noticed that Swede's shoulder was bleeding.

The Norwegian logger caught Birch's surprised look and grinned ruefully. "It's just a scratch. I may not be much of a shot, but I'm very good at running and hiding."

Garrity called down from the driver's seat. "Sure was lucky there weren't any passengers this trip."

Birch said wryly, "Yeah, we're lucky, all right."

CHAPTER 11

SWEDE'S shoulder hurt like the blazes, but he'd endured worse injuries; there was the time he'd gotten pinned under a felled tree. He'd lost all the feeling in his legs. Most of the loggers thought he'd lose his legs, maybe die—but he knew better. After he was dragged out from under the tree, the town doctor wanted to amputate both of his legs. Swede said no. He was determined to walk again. So the doctor put his legs in splints. Later Swede was able to get around on crutches.

At first, Bierbohm wouldn't let him work. But without work, he wasn't getting paid. Without his pay, Greta would never be able to join him in America. He almost had enough saved up. So he convinced his boss to let him work in the kitchen. He stood on his crutches for hours at a time, washing dirty plates and tin cups and serving up the food. In between meals, he practiced walking. At first he relied on his crutches, but soon he was able to lurch around without them.

It took him almost six months to walk again, but he'd done it. And he never wrote a word about his condition to Greta. He didn't want to worry her.

The day he came back to work, everyone in the camp cheered as he walked in. He still had a slight limp, but most people would have to already know about the accident to notice it. And with this payroll, he now had enough money to send for Greta. She would be in America in a few months. He was impatient to see her, impatient for her last letter to arrive from Norway. The next letter he would receive would be from New York, most likely. His brother lived in New York and would meet her when she stepped off the boat.

The bleeding had almost stopped and Swede was careful not to jostle his shoulder too much. A doctor would take care of it as soon as they returned to town.

Swede's thoughts turned to Duke. He hadn't known the swarthy Frenchman for long, but loggers formed fast friendships because of the quick changes in season in the Northwest and the even quicker job changes. The risk involved in logging meant that men were killed or injured just about every day. It happened so frequently that Bierbohm would have been better off with a full-time doctor in the camp. But like most logging camp managers, he couldn't see spending the money when there was a perfectly good doctor ten miles away in Grant's Pass.

Returning to the present, Swede looked around him. Birch was maintaining a stoic silence on the return trip. He could tell that Birch was beating himself up over Duke's death.

When Swede first met Jefferson Birch, he realized that this was a peaceful man, not unlike himself. However, he also became aware of that intangible something in Birch's past that was eating away at him—as if he needed to be in control of every situation. When something happened that was beyond his control, like Duke reaching for a gun in the presence of gun-wielding outlaws, he acted as if he was personally responsible.

Swede glanced over at Wolfgang. He was a mountain of a man with a simplicity about him that was so unlike his hardheaded businesslike father. Wolfgang was also silent during the return trip. But then, it would have been hard to get a word in edgewise with Garrity around.

Bierbohm was waiting in the camp when they arrived. He saw Duke's limp body slung over his saddle and his face grew grim. Swede swung his gaze over to Birch, whose face was an impassive mask. Bierbohm marched over.

"I'm sorry," Birch said. "He was told not to draw his gun."

Bierbohm's face grew red. "Damnation! He was such a hothead! This means more work for the rest of my men. We're already down to an impossibly low number of workers for a logging operation. The risk will be greater now for everyone." The German stared hard at the corpse as if he could will it to get up and work. Then he asked Birch, "Is the money safe?"

Birch raised his eyebrows as if he were thinking, *How can Bierbohm think about business at a time like this?* He just didn't understand a logging operation and the dangers involved. Birch pulled the saddlebags down from Cactus and tossed them to Bierbohm.

As Bierbohm opened the saddlebags' pockets and pulled out the money, he asked, "It's all here?"

Wolfgang answered, "Yes, Papa. We saved the money for you." He looked weary, as if his father's overriding concern for the payroll, as opposed to Duke's death, was a burden for him.

Bierbohm gave Birch a short, satisfied nod as he offered a sum of money in his outstretched hand. "Here is your pay for good work."

Birch's face betrayed revulsion. He waved the money aside. Bierbohm said, "Take it. You deserve it. There will be another bonus when the gang is caught." He shook the money at Birch.

Birch took the money, then turned to Swede and Wolfgang. "Send this to Duke's parents along with whatever money he was owed for work."

Wolfgang nodded.

Bierbohm watched this transaction and shook his head. Then he turned toward his tent with the payroll, presumably to roll in it before doling it out to his workers.

Swede and Birch walked to the meal tent. They sat down at a table with flapjacks and sausages in front of them.

"What's your plan now, Birch?"

The lean hard ex-Ranger looked up at Swede and shrugged. "I don't have a plan. I make it up as I go along."

"Is that what you always do when you're investigating a situation like this—make it up as you go along?"

Birch smiled faintly. "It's the way I was taught. Every situation is different, so I've got to be ready to move in any number of directions."

Swede asked, "Who taught you all of that?"

"I was with the Texas Rangers for a few years."

Swede raised his eyebrows. "The Texas Rangers? That's a well-known outfit. Even my wife, Greta, back in Norway, has heard of them. She will be interested to learn that I have met a Ranger."

"Ex-Ranger," Birch corrected him. "I didn't know they were so popular. I knew we'd gained quite a reputation here in America, but not in the Old World."

"Why wasn't I told about this the other night?" Swede wanted to know.

Birch's faint smile split into a wider grin. "Wasn't any of your damn business then."

They chuckled.

Swede turned onto a more familiar subject. "What about the outlaws? Did you recognize any of them?"

Birch shook his head. "I don't know everyone here in Grant's Pass, but apparently the leader knew enough about me to call me by name. Did you see or hear anything familiar?"

Swede scratched his head. "I'm afraid I was too busy dodging bullets to get a good look. I don't think any of us could say we got a good look at them, could you?"

"Well," Birch said, "the leader used pomade on his hair. His fingernails were soft and clean like he didn't hold up stages for a living. He wore new boots, too. Most outlaws spend so much time on the road that their new boots look old and dusty in a matter of hours." He speared the last sausage on his plate.

Swede shook his head. "I didn't notice any of those things. How could you notice all that while you were being shot at? And what does it mean to an ex-Texas Ranger?"

"It means that the leader wasn't someone who spent a lot of time outdoors—the part of his face that I could see wasn't used to the sun. He was from Grant's Pass because he addressed me by my name. He handled a gun well enough, but I don't think he would have been a very good shot. If he's living in town, he probably doesn't use a gun on a regular basis."

Swede was impressed by the ex-lawman's attention to detail while being held by outlaws. He could only remember staring down a gun's barrel. When Duke reached for his gun, Swede didn't remember Duke's action, he recalled instead the flash of bullet and powder that made his logger friend double over and fall off his horse. How he'd got from sitting on his horse to his position behind the boulder was beyond him; he recalled, however, the drop of cold sweat that ran down his spine the moment after he'd made it to safety behind the rock. He recalled the feeling of relief that followed. But he hadn't felt the bullet passing through his shoulder, nor the blood running down his arm until after it happened.

Swede stood up and said to Birch, "I must clear the skid road before any more logs roll down it today. Will you be staying?"

"No," Birch replied. "I have to get back to town. I have to look into a few things."

Swede went outside, grabbed a mule team, and headed for the skid road. A few minutes later, he caught sight of Birch among the tan oaks, slowly descending the forest path. With the sound of bandsaws biting into wood and loggers shouting instructions at each other, Swede swept the skid road smooth.

CHAPTER 12

IT was another hot sunny day in Grant's Pass. Felix Pierce was carefully shaving the smooth planes of his face and admiring his image in the mirror. For a man in his early forties, he looked ten years younger. He didn't have the worry lines and crow's feet that marked most men's faces at forty. But then, Pierce didn't worry about too many things these days. Life had been good to him so far.

The only bit of unpleasantness had happened the other day on the road to Jacksonville. He frowned briefly at the memory and vowed to be more careful next time.

Pierce turned to more positive thoughts. Things had been going well for him since he came to Grant's Pass a few months ago. Even his saloon was doing better. He'd even made a bit of a profit in the last month, if he included the IOUs incurred by the miners and loggers. *I guess it's true what they say about hard times*, he thought. *People spend more on entertainment to escape their misery.*

A knock outside his bedroom door brought in his maid. He gave her his dusty boots to polish and watched her walk out the door. "She's a nice bit to look at," he told himself. Maybe he could offer her a job in his saloon.

After a fine breakfast and a smoke, Pierce set out to run errands for the day. There was so much to do today. As he strolled down the main street, he greeted Marshal

Stubbs. It just wasn't the same without Carver around. Pierce had taken a liking to Jim, almost like the son he never had. True, the kid had been a hothead, but Pierce had only had experience with daughters. Both of his girls, Annabelle and Madeline, lived back in Connecticut with their mother. He hadn't thought about his wife Esther in several weeks.

His regular payments to Connecticut by Wells Fargo never caused him to pause and miss Esther, although he thought about his daughters frequently. Annabelle would be about fifteen now and Madeline was twelve. He hadn't seen them for almost ten years. He occasionally thought about going back for a visit, or perhaps permanently, if Esther would take him back.

He had a lot of things to do today. One of his first errands was to pay a visit to Meg O'Malley, a visit that he didn't mind making. He wanted her as a lover, but Meg hadn't responded the way he'd hoped she would. She had kept at arm's length whenever he was near; lately, she had been avoiding him altogether. In fact, he had seen her on several occasions with that nosy detective, Jefferson Birch. She looked at Birch the way he wanted her to look at him. He wondered if anything was going on between them. Well, today was the day that he would put an end to that, too.

He walked to the back of Meg's saloon, climbed the stairs, and rapped on the door. After a moment, the door opened a crack and an eye peered out at Pierce. The door opened wider and he stepped in, temporarily blinded by the midmorning sun. Through the rapidly disappearing haze, he saw that he'd been let in by one of Meg's dancing girls, Rosie. She was a tall, willowy creature with chestnut hair that tumbled all around her shoulders.

"You here to see Meg, I suppose." Rosie pulled her robe tightly around her nightgown. "You know your way back." With that, she turned and went into her own room.

Pierce called out a soft, "Thank you," after her closing door and proceeded down the narrow hall. At the end of the hall, he tapped lightly on Meg's door. It was the only door with ornamental carving on it. All the others were made from slabs of tan oak.

Meg was dressed when she opened the door. Pierce was slightly disappointed—he'd wanted to catch her in a state of undress, maybe just after Birch had left. He'd already made up his mind that they were lovers.

Instead, she was dressed in a cream-colored dress with beige lace at the throat and wrists. The effect was feminine but businesslike. A pair of reading glasses lay on her desk next to an account book.

Meg's face betrayed her impatience and dislike of Pierce. "What are you doing here, Felix?"

He pushed the door open wider, Meg stepping back involuntarily. Pierce strode into the room, outwardly oblivious to Meg's brusqueness.

He addressed her. "It's a lovely morning, Meg. You shouldn't be cooped up here in your room. Let's get out and enjoy the sunshine together."

Meg's arms were crossed when he turned to face her. She asked again, "Felix, what are you doing here?"

He replied, "I just came by for a friendly visit."

Meg uncrossed her arms and clasped her hands behind her back. "Well, I appreciate the thought, but I have work to do. I don't have time for a visit." She crossed the room and held the door open for him. He chose not to take the hint.

"You wound me, Meg. You know how I feel about you." Pierce walked to the door and closed it firmly.

"And you know that it's not mutual." Meg had moved away from him, putting a chair and end table between them. Her arms were crossed again, her stance tense.

Pierce knew he was going to go through all the arguments he'd been through before with Meg. "We'd make a good team, you and me. We could become business partners and consolidate the saloons."

"No, thank you."

"I know that you don't like the idea of running a cathouse, but I could take care of that part of the business. I've had experience with whorehouses."

"I bet you have," she said wryly. "But I don't think so, Felix. Please leave."

Pierce stepped closer to her. "Look, Meg. I know you could learn to care for me if you just gave it a chance. Maybe you need a man who's rougher with you. Someone like Birch," he said in a low, menacing voice. He lunged for her, grabbing her arms. She winced and tried to tear herself out of his grasp. The look on her face frightened him.

"Get your hands off me, Pierce." Meg's voice was steady despite her predicament.

Pierce asked urgently, "You've been seeing Birch, haven't you? He's been here, hasn't he?"

"It's none of your business. Please, Felix, you're hurting me."

"Hasn't he?" His voice rose and he shook her. "What have you told him? You're betraying this town, you know."

"No! I haven't done anything. I haven't said anything to him. I hardly know him."

"You knew Birch well enough to go on a buggy ride.

Maybe that's when you told him about me. He suspects me, you know."

An edge of hysteria laced Meg's voice. Or maybe he was imagining it. It made him feel in control either way. She said, "He comes into my saloon for meals. He's taken me for a buggy ride once. I haven't told him anything to make him suspect you, but he's not stupid, Felix. He's probably figured it out for himself or with the help of the miners and the loggers." Meg struggled in his grip, her brilliant blue eyes flashing. "Let go of me. You have no right to treat me this way."

Pierce felt an overwhelming desire for her. He pulled her close and tried to kiss her. Her body seemed to melt when their lips met and his grip on her shoulders relaxed. Suddenly, she pulled away and slapped him. His face tingled where her hand had struck. He touched his reddened jaw.

He looked up at Meg. A derringer had appeared in her hand. It was trained on him.

She said quietly, "Get out of here. I don't want you to come near me again." A few strands of reddish gold hair had escaped from her carefully coiled coiffure during his amorous advances.

Pierce tried to be reasonable. "Meg, put that thing away. There's no need . . ."

She shook her head vigorously. If she was shaken by his actions, she didn't show it. Her aim was steady. "I don't want to have anything more to do with you. I'm going to tell Shorty to shoot you if you so much as set foot in my saloon again."

Pierce slowly backed up, keeping his hands in sight at all times. He had no doubts about Meg's threats—they were real. He had overstepped a boundary. All his life, he'd taken what he wanted, and this time, he wanted Meg and he couldn't have her.

It suddenly occurred to him that Meg might now be a liability. She must have read his thoughts because she said, "And don't worry about Birch. I can handle him. He won't find out anything about your activities from me. I think we can safely guess that most of the townspeople know that you're involved. No one else has said anything, so why should I?"

As he walked away from the Rogue River Saloon, his hands worked furiously, clawing the air as Felix relived the episode in Meg's parlor. The twin emotions, humiliation and fury, swept over him as he headed for the Red Palace. But who was going to pay—Meg O'Malley or the man who was responsible for his shameful actions, Jefferson Birch?

Pierce was beginning to regret his magnanimous testimony on Birch's behalf the night before. The marshal wasn't crazy about a stranger snooping into town business. He'd been ready to throw Birch in jail for Carver's murder, but Pierce had been a witness to the deputy's bullying earlier that day. It was pure coincidence that he had been passing the marshal's house the other evening.

He shook his head in an effort to settle his thoughts into some sort of order. He'd reached the entrance to the Red Palace. Maybe what he needed was a drink.

CHAPTER 13

MEG kept the derringer aimed at the door for a good five minutes before she put the gun down. She kept expecting Felix Pierce to walk back in. Finally, she lowered her newly purchased pistol and placed it back in the little holster pocket that had been specially made for her dresses. She let out a long shaky sigh of relief and sat down on her loveseat.

Would she have used the gun? she mused as she tried to pin renegade strands of hair back into place. Patting her pocket cannon to make sure it was there, she thought about finishing her accounts book but found it too mundane after the scene that had just taken place. It shook her to think that Pierce had been that persistent. She hoped warning him about Shorty would be enough. It frightened her to think about what she knew and how Pierce could use it against her. Then she realized that he had already tried and failed. Somehow, that thought didn't comfort her.

Meg found it hard to take a deep breath. She was still tense after her confrontation with Felix Pierce. While Pierce had been making advances, Meg had felt as if she were watching the whole thing from the ceiling. Now she felt slightly guilty. Pierce kept talking about Birch as if he were her lover, and she certainly didn't find the idea repulsive. However, she knew that it wouldn't be possible. At least not yet. Maybe never. Unless . . .

She came to a decision and strode out the door.

Meg's knock was so faint that at first she thought Birch might not have heard it. He might not be here, she thought. Or if he was here, he might be lying back on his bed, contemplating his next move. She felt her cheeks coloring at her indecent thoughts and raised her hand to knock again. The door opened before her knuckles struck the wood.

When he opened the door, she realized that she was huddled in the doorway, averting her face from the hall as if she didn't want to be recognized. He seemed to realize that something was wrong and brought her into his room immediately.

He smiled apologetically and said, "Sorry this isn't a fancy hotel suite, Meg, but I'm on the sheriff's payroll."

She smiled faintly and said, "I didn't expect it to be. I don't think the Gold Hills Hotel has a suite. It would be a waste of space in the owner's eyes."

"What can I do for you, Meg? You must have a good reason for coming here."

Meg was starting to regret her impulsive visit to Birch. She'd thought she was made of stronger stuff, but now it was clear that telling Birch what she knew would only get them both into more trouble than either of them could handle.

Instead, she said, "I really just came to see how the investigation is going for you."

Birch shot a quizzical look in her direction. "Is that really why you came here?"

She hesitated slightly, then broke into a smile. "Yes."

"Okay. I guess the news will be out soon anyway. I got the loggers' payroll through yesterday."

"That's wonderful." She tried to keep the note of relief out of her voice.

He added, "But it cost a life. I had three loggers from

the camp ride shotgun with me and we were ambushed on the way back. I'd told them not to draw against armed road agents, but one of the loggers, Duke, drew his gun and was killed. He had parents back in France."

Meg suddenly felt sick. She struggled to maintain her calm outward appearance. Why should the death of an unknown logger affect her so much? She tried to brush the feeling aside.

"I'm sorry to hear that." Meg hoped Birch couldn't hear the slight tremor in her voice. Why should she feel guilty for keeping certain information to herself? It was only self-preservation.

"Why are you telling me all of this?" She asked Birch. "I could be one of the people you're looking for."

"You asked me," he said simply, then added, "Besides, I haven't told you anything you couldn't have found out later today."

She turned away from him for a moment, then swung back around to face him. "Birch, tell me the truth. Do you suspect me?"

He laughed. "Do I have reason to suspect you, Meg?" He grew serious. "I don't think so. But I have to warn you that everyone is under suspicion. Why ask me that?"

"I had a visit from someone who thinks that you suspect him and I just wondered." She shrugged.

"Who?"

Meg's eyes wandered around the room as she unconsciously bit her lip. He tried again, this time in a gentler tone. "Look, Meg. If he's not involved, he has nothing to be afraid of."

After a minute, she nodded, resigned. "Felix Pierce asked me." Meg knew she was going to regret this moment of weakness. Maybe Birch would get to Pierce first. It had been a long time, but maybe she'd start praying again.

"Do you think he's involved?"

Meg looked up at Birch and said slowly, "Please don't ask me to answer that. I don't know."

He reached for his hat, which was balanced on one of the bedposts. "Can I walk you back to your saloon, Miss O'Malley?"

"No, please, I'll be fine." She couldn't tell him the real reason for declining. Meg dared not be seen in public with him.

"I'm going that way. And it would be my pleasure."

"Really, I'd rather . . ." She couldn't think of a way to gracefully get out of it. Since the hotel was at one end of the town, she couldn't just tell him that she was going in another direction; everything lay to the east of the Gold Hills Hotel.

He held the door for her and they left together.

Birch walked her to the door of her saloon, then tipped his hat and walked off in the direction of the stables. Meg watched him retreat for a while as she wondered why on earth she had gone up to his room in the first place.

When she stepped into her saloon, her knees suddenly gave out on her. She grabbed the nearest available chair to sit down in before everyone in the place witnessed her collapse. Why had she mentioned Felix Pierce? She had enough troubles with that man without putting Jefferson Birch on Pierce's trail. One thing she was grateful for was that Pierce had not been anywhere in sight as Birch walked her back. She didn't want a visit from him tonight after the saloon closed down.

She caught Shorty's attention and instructed him to

sit down at her table. Then she told him about Pierce's visit and what she wanted him to do if Pierce ever came around uninvited and alone. After Shorty enthusiastically agreed, she felt much better.

CHAPTER 14

"IT'S time to go to Jacksonville, Jake." Carl Ridley eyed the gold nuggets they had amassed in the last few days.

Jake, the other Ridley brother, wiped his hands on the front of his already grimy shirt. He grinned. "Ol' Lije sure bought the right claim, didn't he?"

Carl stooped down and scooped up a handful of nuggets. He let them run through his fingers. "We taking this load to Jacksonville?"

Jake scratched his head. "I don't know if that's such a good idea, Carl. Maybe we should wait till that feller Birch catches them road agents."

"Pah!" Carl stood up, a sour look on his face. "I don't think there's such a thing as a bunch of outlaws getting together to rob folks. If you ask me, it's all a pack of lies made up by the townsfolk to keep us miners from taking our gold away from here. They'd rather that we spend all our dust on drinking and dancing girls instead of using it to buy land and cattle. Besides, I don't trust that Birch feller. I think he's just after gold. He just doesn't want to work for it. He's probably as bad as those outlaws."

"Then why was Elijah Stearns killed? What about the others who have been killed? And why has the logging camp payroll been ambushed?"

Carl paused to try to reason it out. Then he shook his head. "I don't know, Jake. Maybe Elijah and the rest found out that the townsfolk meant to keep them and their gold nuggets here. All I know is that we can't leave this here gold sitting around and we can't mine anymore until we haul this to a bank to be weighed. We gotta go."

Jake ran a hand through his unwashed hair. "Well, I'll go, I guess. I just wonder if it's such a good idea, though. What'll we do if we get ambushed?"

"Look. Elijah left early in the morning and tried to ride through Grant's Pass without anyone seeing him. I guess someone saw him and that's why he's dead. Maybe we shouldn't draw attention to ourselves. Maybe we should go into town, have a drink at the Red Palace or the Rogue River Saloon, then just casually get on our horses and leave town." Carl looked satisfied with his plan, but Jake had a doubtful look on his face.

Jake asked, "But what good will that do? Then everyone will see us leave!"

Carl looked confused for a moment, then brightened. "Yeah, but this way there'll be so many people in town that we can slip away."

"Do you think it's such a good idea for us to go have a drink? You know how you get when you drink, Carl . . ."

"Don't worry about it, kid. Let's load up these nuggets."

Felix Pierce watched the two miners come in. It was unusual for miners to be at the Red Palace this early in the day. But then, maybe they were taking a much needed break. The taller of the two had a long tangled beard and wore a shapeless hat of an indeterminate color. The other one was stocky with shaggy hair and he wore a grimy vest over a grimy shirt.

The tall one ordered two beers and they stood by the bar. Pierce couldn't put his finger on it, but he had a hunch that he should talk to them. He got up and motioned to his bartender.

"Dusty, don't let these two gentlemen pay for their drinks. And make it a bottle of our finest whiskey."

The two men looked over at Pierce; both men had surprised expressions, but the taller man's expression changed to suspicion a moment later. "You don't have to do that, mister," he said grudgingly. The bottle of whiskey arrived and he looked thirstily at it. "We can pay our own way."

"Nonsense," Pierce said expansively. "I own this place and I can do anything I damn well please. And I just decided to give you a drink on the house."

The tall man had already grabbed the bottle by the neck and partook of the libation greedily. The short one hesitated, then poured out a portion of the amber liquid. Both men stared at their whiskey as if they could drink it with their eyes.

"Drink up, gentlemen," Pierce urged. "Don't be shy."

The first drinks went down and with the second ones, Pierce was urged to join them. He learned that they were brothers, Carl and Jake Ridley. With the third round, he learned that they were from Kansas and had come out here several years ago when the fever struck them. By the fourth round, they told him that they'd just latched onto a very promising claim, and after the fifth and sixth drinks, Carl told him about their plans to bring their first haul up to Jacksonville.

Pierce excused himself for a moment, ostensively to relieve himself, but once out of sight, he took care of another matter. When he returned, the brothers were having an argument.

"Carl!" Jake, the short one, tugged at his brother's sleeve in annoyance. "You've had too much. Let's go."

His face had gone white. He held his liquor better than his elder brother. His hands were steady and he had acquired a cautious look in his eye after Carl had let their plans slip.

"But Jake," Carl slurred, "this is our compadre."

Pierce winced. If there was one thing he hated, it was a sloppy drunk who became overfamiliar with him. He smiled reassuringly.

Carl had turned to him. "You won't tell on us, will you? We're leaving right after I have one more drink." He reached for the bottle, but Jake moved it out of the way.

"You've had enough, Carl. You'll be no good to me if we get ambushed."

While Jake was scolding his elder brother, Pierce poured another shot and gave it to Carl before Jake could stop him.

Jake glared at him. "What are you doing, trying to get him to the point where I have to tie him to his horse? He'll be no good now on the trip up there."

Pierce frowned on the outside, but he was glowing inside at the thought of all that gold. "I apologize. I guess I saw how good your brother was feeling and I just helped it along a bit." He spread his hands in a helpless gesture. "I own a saloon, you know, and it's just natural to keep the whiskey flowing. I'm sure you won't have any trouble on your way up there. I don't see what harm can be done by telling me about your good fortune."

Jake shook his head as if to shake off his alcoholic haze. "Maybe you're right. But then, maybe we were overheard by someone connected to the road agents. All I know is that we got to get on the road." He pushed himself away from the bar and grabbed his brother by an elbow and steered him toward the door. He paused at the door and turned to address Pierce. "Thanks for the drinks, Mr. Pierce. We'll stop in when we come back." Then they were gone.

Pierce smiled and thought, *You'll see me sooner than you think.*

He stepped outside long enough to watch Jake and Carl Ridley ride away. Jake was too busy trying to keep Carl from falling off his horse for either of them to notice that Pierce had tied yellow bandannas to the right side of their saddles. Pierce hoped that one of his men would spot the kerchiefs and follow the brothers. Maybe he'd join the fun later.

CHAPTER 15

THE ride to the mining camp seemed faster in the daytime, and truth be told, it probably was. There wasn't the feeling that Birch had to tread carefully in cold virgin moonlight with darkness just outside, ready to close in when the first cloud passed over the moon. Sunlight streamed in through the trees. It glinted off the Rogue River like the gleam of a polished nickel-plated gun.

When Birch arrived, he dismounted outside the camp and walked in. He hadn't expected to see any of the miners there, so he wasn't surprised to see only women and children carrying out the daily duties that kept the camp running.

Several women were looking after the children while the rest were performing perfunctory duties—washing clothes and dishes, cleaning and stoking the campfire, preparing the next meal. Luke Stone's wife was mending a shirt when she saw Birch approaching. She put her mending down and stood up to greet him. Other women and children in the camp had stopped their chores to watch the stranger's approach.

"Mr. Birch! Luke is at the claim with our sons." She had a pleasant voice and beneath her weathered face was a woman who had been attractive, even pretty, in her youth. "Can I bring you coffee?"

He shook his head. "No, thank you, Mrs. Stone."

"Please call me Lucille." She reached up with a cal-

119

loused hand and smoothed some of the wisps of hair that had come loose in the hot morning sun. "Did you want to talk to Luke or one of the other men? I can take you to their claim."

"I just came up to check on the miners. Have they agreed to organize yet? Has your husband talked any sense into them?"

Lucille Stone shook her head helplessly. "I'm afraid it's a lost cause. Very few miners are willing to trust the others."

"Has anyone talked about taking a haul up to Jacksonville alone?"

She thought for a moment. "I don't think anyone has mentioned it."

A young girl of about ten years of age was tugging at Lucille Stone's skirts and the woman bent down. The girl had a thin reedy voice as she addressed the two adults. "I saw the Ridley brothers leave the camp this morning. They had big bulging saddlebags."

"Where were they headed, Sally?" Mrs. Stone bent closer to the girl.

"They were headed toward town."

Birch asked Sally, "When did they leave?"

Sally scrunched up her face in concentration. "It was sometime after breakfast. They went out to their claim for a while, then came back here for something. Then they went away."

Lucille straightened up and looked at Birch. He nodded briefly to her and thanked Sally solemnly. She returned a friendly grin and left to play with the other children.

Lucille said, "What does that mean?"

"Are the Ridley brothers inclined to go to Grant's Pass just for a drink or for supplies?"

She replied, "No. Carl likes to drink, but since they got Elijah Stearns's claim, they work it steadily. They go into town on Saturday nights like the rest of the miners. As for getting supplies, we send a wagon in with a list of supplies once a month and the miners take turns going into town and missing a day of mining. The Ridleys know that they can borrow from anyone in the camp if they need something between supply visits."

"Have they talked about how much gold they've mined on the claim?" Birch already knew the answer to this, but he asked more out of a sense of duty.

Lucille Stone shook her head and smiled. "No one talks about their luck, good or bad. After living in this camp together for all these years, we get an idea of who's doing well and who's not, but even that's not always accurate."

She went on to explain that some miners are misers even when they hit a strike and others are more honest and will pay their fair share no matter how little gold dust they've panned.

"Of course, in the case of the Ridley brothers, Jake is close-mouthed about their fortune, but Carl drinks. And when he drinks, he talks, like a lot of these men."

Something in Lucille Stone's eyes told Birch that she wasn't just referring to men in general, but to her own husband.

He asked her, "Has Carl been talking?"

"I can only tell you what I've heard around the camp. A lot of rumors fly around, too, you know. Ever since they got Stearns's claim, they've been trying to find the spot where Lije struck gold. Miners who strike tend to cover up their motherlode so when they're not around the claim, a stranger can't just come in and mine a little for himself," she said. "I guess they found the strike because a few nights ago, Carl and Luke and a couple of others started drinking here in camp and, well, Carl let it slip that he and Jake found it. It was pure luck that Jake overheard Carl and dragged his brother away before he gave away where the motherlode was."

Birch's face grew stern as he listened. He nodded and thanked Luke's wife for her information. "I'm going back and see if I can find the Ridley brothers on the Jacksonville road. When Luke comes back for supper, please tell him what you and I worked out."

Her face radiated pride, as if a sense of her own importance wasn't a feeling that happened to her often. Birch felt a surge of kindness for the woman before him. Luke Stone had recounted some of their hardships, but Birch could see the years of living outdoors in her face. Traveling across country in a covered wagon and several years of living in a shack by a river had left her faded and weary.

Although the winters were fairly mild here in southern Oregon, the sun was strong all summer long. Torrential rains passed over the Siskiyou Mountains and flooded the valley, causing the Rogue River to overflow in the springtime as well. There was enough variety in the seasons not only to erode the land but the people too.

And all the gold nuggets mined by their husbands couldn't bring rosy cheeks and creamy complexions back to the women who stood by them in their gold fever and who bore their children.

She was probably his age because her children were about twelve and fourteen years old. If Birch hadn't married late, he would have had children about the

same age as the Stone children. Before thoughts of
Audrey brought on that familiar feeling, Birch mounted
Cactus, thanked Lucille again, and rode off in search of
the Ridley brothers.

CHAPTER 16

THINGS had been fairly quiet this afternoon in Grant's Pass for Henry Stubbs. He'd kept close to his daily schedule in the vain hope that everything was settled down for good. He didn't like to lose deputies and he didn't like to deal with death.

No one had come in asking for the deputy's job yet, but it didn't worry Stubbs at all. Someone would turn up eventually, either a miner who was sick of panning river silt or a logger who wanted steady pay. It didn't matter if he had experience or if he could even find the right end of a gun as long as he was a warm body.

As the marshal thought more about it, a logger would be better because most of those fellows were strong. A logger wouldn't have the back problems a miner would have and could probably tackle a mean drunk better than a puny miner. Yeah, a logger would have it over a miner any day.

From his window, which overlooked the street, he saw Felix Pierce striding toward his office. A moment later, the Red Palace owner was sitting on the other chair in Stubbs's office.

"You look like a man with a purpose today, Felix."

Pierce smiled. "I'll be riding up to Jacksonville soon, Henry. Maybe you could keep an eye on the saloon for me."

The scent of pomade permeated the stuffy little office. Henry's nose twitched. He didn't like those flowery toiletries for men. Men should smell like old leather and dust. Despite Pierce's preference for pomade, he was a good man, so Stubbs ignored the smell.

Stubbs swung his boots onto his desktop and tilted his chair back. He rocked the precariously balanced chair back and forth. He could tell that this bothered Pierce because his hands began to worry each other unconsciously.

"Sure I will," Stubbs replied expansively. "You coming back tonight?"

Pierce got up and walked to the door. He paused and said, "Oh, yes. I shouldn't be too long."

Stubbs looked out his window a few minutes later and saw Birch riding into town on his horse. The marshal decided now was as good a time as any to talk to Birch and stepped outside to flag him down.

Birch looked exasperated and harried. He reluctantly led his horse over to Stubbs. "What do you want, Marshal?" he asked in a peeved tone.

"Come down off that horse and come inside," Stubbs said. He took out a cigar and explained, "We need to talk about your progress. I just got a wire from the sheriff asking about you."

Birch grimaced and shook his head. "It'll have to wait, Marshal. Two miners started out for Jacksonville a while ago and I have to catch up to them." He wheeled his mount onto the street.

"Wait a minute, Birch, damn it!" Stubbs gestured with his unlit cheroot in protest. "Come back here now. Those miners have to be out of this jurisdiction by now."

Birch smiled and shrugged. "But my jurisdiction is the Jacksonville road. And if I'm going to have anything to report to Calhoun, I have to follow the Ridley brothers' trail."

With that, he spurred his horse into a gallop, leaving Stubbs to inhale a puff of dust.

Stubbs muttered, "Damn!" then lit his cheroot.

CHAPTER 17

JAKE began to wonder if it had been such a good idea. He knew that Carl fancied himself the brains in their family, but his brains turned to mush if he came within ten feet of sour mash or whiskey. He'd stopped at the Rogue River Saloon and pumped three cups of strong hot coffee into Carl, but that hadn't seemed to help much. The truth of the matter was that without Jake to look out for him, Carl, for all his brains, would be just another poor old sop in this boom town. Jake was his conscience. And it was Jake who suggested that they file for Elijah Stearns's claim before anyone else beat them to it Jake was the one who spent all day and half the night for a week looking for Stearns's hidden motherlode.

Now they were traveling down this sidewinder road to weigh their gold and bank some of it. It was true that some miners just kept on mining and spending their dust without ever going to Jacksonville to weigh it, but none of those miners wanted to put it in a bank either. They mined just enough to make it to the next panning. Dust was the accepted form of money in these parts. Even most of the loggers would trade in their month's wages, paid out in bank notes, for a poke. A poke was a small purse filled with gold dust.

Jake eyed the landscape ahead of them, looking for an ambush. When Carl was sober he had a quicker eye than Jake. He looked over at his inebriated brother and rage welled up inside. How could Carl be so reckless with liquor? It was frustrating to know that the only thing between getting to Jacksonville in one piece and being ambushed and killed for their gold was his sobriety. He had taken Carl's gun away without his brother's knowledge. One thing more dangerous than a sober man with a gun was a pie-eyed man with a gun.

A sharp high gibbering accompanied by rustling leaves distracted Jake. He pulled out his gun and cocked it, swinging it wildly from left to right before he realized that it had only been a couple of birds squabbling in a tree.

"Wha' was that?" his brother slurred. He grabbed for his gun and found his holster empty. "Say, Jake. I must have left my gun back at the camp."

"We'll get you a gun in Jacksonville," Jake assured him. "You're drunk as a skunk and shouldn't even be allowed on a horse in your state, let alone carry a gun."

Carl took offense. "What do you mean I'm drunk as a skunk? I've never even seen a drunk skrunk." He guffawed at his clever thought.

"You don't handle a gun so well," his brother pointed out, "when you've been drinking."

Carl's head wobbled from side to side as if it were on a spring rather than on his neck. "I can shoot a gun better when I've been drinking than you can when you're sober. You couldn't even shoot a tin can on a fence if you were a foot away. Give me your gun. I'll protect us."

"No."

Carl leaned over toward his brother, making a swipe at Jake's holster. He started to slide off his horse. Jake grabbed him by his left shoulder and pushed Carl back up on his saddle. Carl had a strange look on his face.

Jake asked, "What's the matter?"

"Did you buy any funny-colored bandannas just before we left Grant's Pass?"

Carl's brother snorted. "I thought you said you were in good enough shape to handle a gun if we were ambushed. Now you're telling me that you don't even know what we did in Grant's Pass."

"I know where we were," Carl snapped. "You have a yellow bandanna tied to the side of your saddle. Did Meg O'Malley give it to you when you were pouring coffee down my gullet?"

Jake looked back and sure enough, a yellow bandanna was tied to his saddle. He reached down and untied it. He sniffed it for perfume.

Carl said, "Maybe one of those dance hall girls likes you. What was the name of that girl you danced with last week, the one with the apple red cheeks who giggled almost the whole time you waltzed her around the dance floor?"

Jake grinned. "Emmeline. I must have spent almost my whole poke on her." He shook his head. "You know how strict Meg O'Malley is with those girls. Emmeline wouldn't have done this."

Carl shrugged. "I don't think Meg O'Malley has much say over what her girls do when they're not working. It's not as if she has to protect their reputations. Maybe Emmeline wants to marry you. She could do worse."

"Yeah," Jake said. "She could have wanted to marry *you*." Jake looked up from fixing his new necktie to see his brother scouting the area ahead. Carl seemed to have sobered up enough over the last few minutes to be trusted with his gun again. Then he spotted something on his brother's saddle. "Hey, Carl! What's that bit of yellow tied on the right side of *your* saddle?"

It was then that they heard the rustle of leaves, and they knew it wasn't the sound of birds squabbling in a tree this time.

"Throw down your guns and gold and be damned quick about it!"

Felix Pierce never tired of saying that line in a gruff, unrecognizable voice from behind his mask. He enjoyed the looks on his victims' faces as they obeyed his command grudgingly. He felt an incredible rush of power every time.

Pierce had been able to catch up easily. Jake and Carl Ridley had made little progress on the road to Jacksonville because of their inebriated state. Pierce's lookout man had indeed spotted the yellow bandannas just outside of town and had gone on ahead to gather up some men. A little less than fifteen minutes later, Pierce met with four members of the large network of outlaws that he commanded. They stalked the miners until Pierce gave the signal to ambush.

After relieving the Ridleys of their gold, Pierce and his gang would divide it up in their mountain hideout and he would go back to Grant's Pass to protect his sterling reputation. After all, someone had to join the posse and lead the good citizens astray. In fact, after that last miner was killed, Pierce had been the first volunteer to be deputized. He'd led a band of men as far as Klamath Falls before giving up the chase. It had earned him some aches and pains from riding so hard that day, but he took it easy that night, leaving his saloon in the capable hands of his bartender and chief bouncer, Dusty.

Volunteering to lead a posse had been good for business that night. All the posse members dropped by the Red Palace and drank the place dry.

He'd make sure that what had happened to the last miner wouldn't happen today. Of course, he hadn't been in charge of that ambush, but it had taught him to be careful about securing his mask so it wouldn't slip at an unfortunate moment.

The Ridley brothers' faces were grim as they dropped their guns and unlaced the bags of nuggets from their saddles. The older brother—Pierce couldn't remember which was which—was having a little trouble with his ties. His fingers must have been numb and stiff from drinking.

Pierce gestured impatiently with his gun. "Hurry it up, you on the right."

The bags finally dropped to the road with a soft thud. Two of Pierce's men dismounted to gather up their booty.

CHAPTER 18

BIRCH rode hard through the twists and turns of the Jacksonville road. He remembered the road from having ridden shotgun just a few days before, and it was a damned good thing, too. He could break Cactus's leg on this road if he wasn't careful, but he had to catch up to the Ridleys. Maybe he could prevent another ambush. The terrain was too rocky and unpredictable for him to take a chance leading Cactus off the road. There was too much mountainous country, submerged rocks, and rattlesnakes basking in the sun near boulders for Birch to try a subtle approach. If he came upon the ambushers, it would have to be head on.

And that's exactly what happened. He rounded a bend and saw the outlaw band about a quarter of a mile away. He could see that the Ridleys had already been fleeced of their gold. The outlaw leader turned around, aimed at Birch, and fired a shot. Birch pulled his gun and spurred Cactus on. He shouted at the top of his lungs to distract the outlaws as he aimed his Colt at them.

The two outlaws with the gold dropped the bags in surprise, their eyes wide with fear at this crazy man coming toward them. Two other road agents shot at him and missed. It was hard to aim accurately at a rapidly moving figure. A fifth outlaw took cover behind some trees.

The two Ridley brothers sat on their horses for a

moment, blinking in surprise at this turn of events.
Then Jake took action by slipping off his saddle and
grabbing their guns. He tossed one of the guns to his
brother, Carl, who had also dismounted, and they took
cover in some brush on the side of the road.

In the meantime, Birch veered off within range of
the shooting and abandoned Cactus near a tree, pausing
only to grab a length of rope. He stationed himself
behind some undergrowth that afforded him a view of
the road. By this time, the outlaws had taken cover as
well. Two of the horses had run off and the bags of gold
lay in the middle of the road, unattended but with many
eyes coveting them from various hidden positions along
the road.

Birch noticed that the Ridley brothers had separated
and that the smaller one was on his side of the road. He
would try to get over to him and together they could
cover each other. He knew that there was at least one
outlaw between them and he would have to eliminate
that problem.

The shooting was intermittent, and in the silences,
the leader shouted threats to the brothers.

"Give up and we'll let you live!" was one of the offers.

Birch saw a flash of red beyond the bushes to his left.
He crept stealthily along, his boots making as little noise
as possible. Soon he had a clear view of the road agent
stationed behind a tree with his back to Birch. He was
taking wild shots at moving bushes, trying not to shoot
a member of his gang.

Birch started toward him.

When Birch was about five feet from jumping him,
the man in the red shirt turned around. He was just a
young kid, about Carver's age, and he had a panicked
look in his eye. He waved the gun wildly at Birch, but

the ex-Ranger ignored it and dove for his gun arm. A
shot went off, but Birch wrestled the gun away, wound
up his right arm, and delivered a roundhouse punch to
the kid's jaw that knocked him out.

He took the bullets out of the unconscious outlaw's
gun chamber and flung the gun away into the bushes.
Then he tied the boy's hands behind his back with some
rope and left him there.

Just as he was ready to continue his mission, he was
jumped from behind and knocked face down. An arm
gripped him across the throat, and for a minute Birch
thought he would be shot. A raspy voice said, "Now
there's only them two miners left to deal with."

Birch didn't feel any cold metal against his head or
neck, so he took a chance and reached up. He grabbed
his attacker by the scruff of the neck and pulled him
forward with a mighty tug.

Birch sprang up, ready to fight. The man he faced
was about one and a half times his own weight. The big
man had bounced back from being thrown and was
circling Birch.

He noted that his opponent wasn't wearing a gun.
Either he'd lost it in the fracas, or he intimidated people
with his size instead. The first blow came to his face and
stunned him. His opponent had lightening fists; he
hadn't seen the wind up and punch. He was slightly
dazed from it, but he covered for it by taking the big
man by surprise and throwing his shoulder at the man's
center of gravity.

The big man staggered and while he tried to recover,
Birch hit him twice in the stomach. His opponent
groaned, but grabbed Birch's arms with a steel grip and
they grappled for a minute. Birch managed to throw
the outlaw to the ground and get another few punches

in, but the man came back with three hits to Birch's stomach that left him unable to breath for a minute.

During that time, his attacker ran over to the young boy and untied him. By the time Birch got his breath back, both outlaws had commandeered two horses standing by the side of the road. He watched with frustration as they made their escape in the direction of Jacksonville. He had no doubt that they would manage to disappear long before they reached the town.

Two of the remaining three outlaws were pinned down by the Ridley brothers. Birch watched as one man made a desperate break for the horses while the third one covered him.

Carl Ridley took aim and shot. The escaping outlaw spun around, then crumpled to the ground like an abandoned marionette.

Birch suddenly realized that he'd lost track of the leader. Fortunately, while Carl kept his gun trained on the remaining outlaw, Birch followed the sound of gunfire across the road.

Birch joined Jake behind a boulder. He knew who the leader was by this time. If the pomade hadn't given him away, his expensive boots would have. Birch stayed Jake's hand from returning gunfire.

"Come on out, Pierce," Birch called. "It's over. I have to take you in."

There was silence for a minute. Then a voice said, "I'm not going in. Let me go quietly."

"You know that's not possible," Birch said reasonably. "You can't just go back to your saloon. The miners and loggers will have a little necktie party. Let me bring you into Jacksonville. The county sheriff will protect you and see that you get a fair trial."

"No," Pierce said. "I want to go to the Grant's Pass

jailhouse. I know Stubbs. He'll be fair with me. I don't know Sheriff Calhoun."

Birch scratched his day's growth in thought. He knew that Calhoun would be fair, but he supposed it was a reasonable request since Felix Pierce knew Stubbs's reputation for not wanting trouble.

He agreed to Pierce's request. "Okay, I'll turn you over to Marshal Stubbs. Now throw out your gun, Pierce," he called. "You're my prisoner now."

A Smith & Wesson landed with a thud on the dirt road, raising a lazy puff of dust. Birch was the first one out on the road.

"Raise your hands above your head and step out slowly from that tree."

Birch kept his gun trained on Pierce's shadowy form. The owner of the Red Palace obeyed Jefferson Birch's instructions. He had pulled his bandanna off and he had a stiff expression on his face, a look more of embarrassment than fear.

Birch noted this with curiosity. Most outlaws that Birch had arrested wore defiant expressions. Pierce's hands were fastened to the saddlehorn of his horse. Birch used the rope left from the kid's escape. He carefully tied the horse's reins to a nearby tree and walked over to the Ridley brothers.

The tall Ridley eyed him with suspicion. The other one nodded. "Thanks." He reached into one of the bags, pulled out a couple of good-sized nuggets, and handed them to Birch. The former Texas Ranger waved the reward away.

Instead, he motioned to their horses, miraculously still nearby. "I'd appreciate it if you'd just answer a question for me."

"Anything," was the reply of the less truculent brother.

"Did anything unusual happen to you on the way through Grant's Pass, or did you tell anyone about your plans?"

The tall one flushed and looked away. The other brother said, "Well, we stopped for a drink at Pierce's saloon—Carl here likes to drink. I should have insisted that we go straight through. But we did stop and after a few drinks, Pierce knew where we were going and why."

Birch nodded perfunctorily. He was about to turn away when Carl added, "There was one strange thing, though. We found these yellow bandannas tied to our saddles. When I found the one on Jake's saddle, we thought it had been tied there by Emmeline. She works for Miss O'Malley. But we found another one tied to my saddle and now . . ." He drifted off, not really sure what conclusion to draw.

Birch looked over at Pierce. The man was slumped in his saddle and didn't appear to be willing to talk.

Jake interrupted Birch's train of thought. "We really should give you a reward for helping us out back there." He held out a small bag of nuggets.

Birch declined again. "Just stand me for a couple of drinks some night. I'm just doing my job."

They nodded, obviously relieved to have recovered their gold without paying an expensive reward.

CHAPTER 19

AFTER consulting each other, Jake and Carl Ridley decided to postpone their trip to Jacksonville until the rest of the gang was captured. Their reasoning was that the escaped outlaws might be waiting to ambush them again further up the road. Most of Pierce's men had headed toward Jacksonville. The Ridley brothers accompanied Jefferson Birch and his prisoner back to Grant's Pass. The captor and captive rode in silence for a mile or two before Pierce said, "Marshal Stubbs will never believe you. I'm respected in Grant's Pass."

Birch shot an amused look at Pierce. "I think the testimonies of Carl and Jake will convince the marshal that you're not as respectable as you appear."

Pierce frowned. He brooded on this for a few minutes, then muttered unhappily, "I know what you're thinking, but you can't prove that I tied those bandannas to their saddles. I'll be out of jail before you report my involvement to the sheriff in Jacksonville."

Carl Ridley responded harshly. "I think you'll be strung up before sundown, Pierce." The effects of his drinking had almost worn off since they had been ambushed. A strong desire for revenge glinted in his bloodshot eyes. "I'll see to it personally."

Birch glanced at Felix Pierce. He had all the trappings of a successful man of the West: carefully trimmed hair, shiny lizardskin boots, custom tailored shirt. But beneath his veneer of self-confidence was a glimmer of fear at Carl Ridley's threats.

Birch looked over at Carl. His set jaw and straight-ahead stare suggested that it wouldn't be easy to talk him out of throwing a hanging party for Felix Pierce. Nevertheless, Birch took a stab at it.

"Wouldn't you get more satisfaction out of attending his trial and having the circuit judge pronounce Pierce guilty?"

Carl looked at Birch with disdain. "What would you know about it, mister? You're not even from around here. You didn't know the miners who were killed by this—this . . ."

His brother quietly interrupted. "I think Birch is right, Carl."

Carl looked at his brother as if he were a traitor.

Jake continued, "No, no, think about it. Either way Pierce will hang. If we do it the legal way, there won't be anyone snooping around afterward."

Felix Pierce's face was pale and damp after listening to the Ridley brothers argue over how and when he should be killed.

"Now look," Pierce said to them. "I didn't have anything to do with the deaths of those men."

Birch and the Ridleys swung around in their saddles to look at him. Birch spoke first. "If you didn't, then who did?"

The outlaw leader's hands were shaking. He looked at the road ahead—maybe he was having second thoughts about Grant's Pass.

He shook his head. "I can't tell you. If we just turn around and head back to Jacksonville now, I'll tell you everything."

Birch took his hat off and ran a sinewy hand through

his hair. He looked over at the Ridley brothers. They both wore frowns.

Birch asked, "What do you think, Carl? Jake?"

Jake scratched the back of his neck thoughtfully. "I don't rightly trust this man."

Carl added, "I agree with Jake. It could be a trap. Maybe we'll be ambushed again on the way to Jacksonville. The rest of his gang all escaped and headed that way. Why should we turn around on his say so?"

Birch mulled it over for a moment. When he was first captured, Pierce insisted on being taken to Grant's Pass because, he said, he would be treated fairly there. Now he was offering to tell Birch everything he knew if they turned around and headed for Jacksonville. Birch wondered what had changed Pierce's mind. Maybe the thought of all those miners and loggers lined up outside the jailhouse with a rope had something to do with it. Even Stubbs would have a hard time protecting Felix Pierce from an angry mob.

The sun was getting low in the sky. Birch's thoughts turned to the escaped road agents, Pierce's men. They might still be watching the road. It would be a greater risk to travel to Jacksonville now. They were only a mile outside of Grant's Pass.

Pierce ran a dry tongue over dry lips. "I wasn't the one who killed those miners, Birch."

Birch came to a decision. "Tell you what, Pierce. You want to go to Jacksonville so bad, I'll escort you there." The relief on Felix Pierce's face was obvious. Birch added, "But you'll have to spend the night in the Grant's Pass jail. We'll start first thing in the morning."

Pierce looked stricken. His face was drained of what little color he had left. "No," he protested, "that won't do at all. It has to be now. I can't go back to Grant's Pass now. Not after what I've just told you . . ."

They were on the edge of town. Pierce looked fearfully one way, and then the other. Jake and Carl snickered at his discomfort.

"I think he's just trying to confuse you, Birch," Carl said. "Like I said before, I bet his cronies are waiting for us to arrive at some ravine further down the Jacksonville road."

Jake said, "Watch your back tonight, Birch. If you want company tomorrow, we'll be glad to go with you. After all, we do have to get this gold to the bank anyway."

"I'll let you fellows know when I'm leaving tomorrow."

The Ridleys rode on ahead. They still had a few miles to go before they were safely ensconced in their camp for the night.

Just before they reached Stubbs's office, Pierce turned and said in a low voice, "My offer still stands if you get me safely to Jacksonville tomorrow."

They reached the marshal's office and Birch dismounted. He unloaded Pierce and guided him inside.

Henry Stubbs must have been watching from the window. He didn't look surprised to see them, but he had a strange look on his face when Felix Pierce's hands were being untied.

Stubbs wore a deep frown. "Well, Birch, what's going on here? You can't just tie up one of the leading citizens of Grant's Pass and waltz in here."

Pierce rubbed his chaffed wrists, his head lowered so his expression couldn't be easily read. Birch told Stubbs the entire story, leaving out that the reason Pierce was being moved to Jacksonville tomorrow was that he would be divulging information on his outlaw pals.

Birch expected he'd have some argument from the marshal since Pierce paid part of Stubbs's wages. It seemed to Birch that since he came here to Grant's Pass, he had spent too much time trying to convince Henry Stubbs that his actions were reasonable and necessary. So when no argument was forthcoming, Birch was more than a little surprised.

"Right. Good work, Birch." Stubbs stood up and grabbed his key ring, fishing around for the right key to unlock one of the three cells in back. "I'll stay here tonight with Pierce just to make sure he doesn't escape."

It was hard to picture Pierce trying to escape. He was shaking like a leaf when he was ushered into his cell. Birch also had a hard time believing that a dandy like Felix Pierce was the wily and ferocious leader of an organized outlaw gang. While he'd obviously been giving the orders during the Ridley's hold-up, it was an amateur job, not the work of a professional. And Birch didn't think Felix Pierce had the eyes of a killer.

Could there be another source planted in this town— or perhaps up in the logging camp? Birch thought long and hard about Bierbohm. Would it really be so terrible if the logging operation was shut down and Bierbohm were out of a job if he'd been stealing the last few months of payrolls? He was in the perfect position. His son, Wolfgang, was the one who picked up the payroll from Grant's Pass. Nothing would prevent him from ambushing the stagecoach on the Jacksonville road earlier in the day and hiding it before going into Grant's Pass to wait for the news that the stage had been held up.

Stubbs accompanied Birch back to his office, shaking

his head. "I really have to hand it to you, Birch. I didn't think it was possible that there was an organized gang, and I certainly didn't think that one of our most respected citizens was involved, let alone turning out to be the leader!"

Birch was going to explain that he had reservations about Pierce as the leader of the whole gang, but he decided not to let Stubbs in on his hunches yet. Instead, he told the marshal that he would be at the jailhouse tomorrow morning after breakfast to pick up his prisoner.

CHAPTER 20

THAT night news of Felix Pierce's arrest swept through the town. Meg did not know how the information had traveled so fast, but it seemed to be good for business. She surveyed her saloon with satisfaction. Loggers and miners were making rounds of all the saloons in town, even the Red Palace. In fact, Felix's saloon was doing more business than the Rogue River Saloon & Gambling Parlor and Stinky's together. She guessed that people went to the Red Palace more out of curiosity than anything else.

Meg's saloon had an air of celebration about it tonight. She had to admit that she was relieved to hear that Felix Pierce was safely behind bars—at least for tonight. She had been told that Birch would pick Pierce up tomorrow morning and escort him to Jacksonville to await trail.

A man stepped through the saloon doors. A hush fell over the room. Jefferson Birch looked weary and bruised.

Someone called out, "His drinks are on me, Shorty. Don't keep the well dry!"

A cheer rose up from the miners and loggers who swarmed around Birch. As he made his way to the bar, the crowd of well-wishers parted for him, clapping him on the back or pumping his hand as he passed. The piano started up again, playing a fast waltz. Meg's girls crowded around Birch in an effort to get him out on

147

the dance floor. Meg was curious to hear what her girls were proposing to Jefferson Birch, so she moved within earshot.

"Come on, Mr. Birch," Rosie was saying as she tugged at his sleeve. "You're entitled to a little fun. You do dance, don't you? I won't charge you."

Birch looked like he was trying to keep a straight face as another girl, Minnie, sidled up to him and said, "Pay no attention to her, sir. Rosie can't waltz to save her life. She'll step all over your toes. I'll dance with you."

Rosie looked miffed at the light-hearted insult. "Well, at least I'll dance with him for free."

Minnie retorted, "And a good thing, too. Who wants to be charged for sore toes?" With an impish smile she turned back to Birch and added, "I wasn't going to charge you either."

Still a third, Oona, elbowed Rosie aside and boldly took his hand without a word. Meg looked on in amusement.

He was saying, "Really, girls, I appreciate the . . ." when Meg caught his eye. "Excuse me, ladies." He extended his hand and she took it.

Presently, they were sailing around the floor, her rust-colored silk gown billowing out like a leaf caught by an autumn wind. He was a smooth dancer, much better than she had expected.

His eyes burned into hers. She felt an uncomfortable warmth rising to her cheeks. She'd had lovers before; men had always pursued her. But once a man became her lover, she controlled the affair. When the passion cooled, she would end the liaison.

Jefferson Birch had proven to be polite and aloof without the passion that usually leads to the pursuit of a woman. Still, she felt that he was as drawn to her as she was to him—or was it all wishful thinking?

The waltz ended. Meg began to pull away from him, but his arms held her fast. Another melody began and in order to maintain some dignity with all eyes upon her in her own establishment, she gave in and enjoyed the next dance. It was a schottische this time and she carefully avoided his eyes as much as possible in such close proximity.

He asked her, "Are you happy it's over?"

She nodded. "I think the mood in here tonight should tell you everything you need to know."

"Do you think I caught the right man?"

She lowered her eyes as if she were concentrating on her feet. She missed a step from concentrating too hard. "Everyone else seems to think so. You did catch him in the act of robbing those two miners. That's pretty damning evidence."

Birch was silent until the schottische ended. Meg got the impression that he wanted to talk more about Pierce to her, but she was too upset by her previous encounter with Pierce to talk about it.

She was about to make an excuse to get away from him when they were thankfully interrupted by Luke Stone. He looked respectfully at Meg, tipped his hat to her, and said, "Excuse me, ma'am. I'd like to buy this gentleman a drink."

Birch looked at Meg for a moment, thanked her for the dance, and headed for the bar with Stone. Meg caught sight of Swede and Gustav Bierbohm's son, Wolfgang, walking toward Birch. For a moment, relief flooded over her because she wouldn't have to talk with Birch about Felix Pierce tonight.

She started making a round of the floor, making sure

that customers were happy. A happy customer meant more money to her. She caught sight of Birch across the room again. Their eyes met briefly. Her heart seemed to catch in her throat as she realized that this might be the last night she'd see him. His work, for all intents and purposes, was finished here.

She began to regret her impulse on the dance floor to be free of him. Maybe she should have talked to him about what was really going on here in Grant's Pass. It would have kept him here longer. She shook the thought right out of her head. That was ridiculous. It would only put them both in more danger. Even though she knew Shorty would protect her from harm, and that Birch would probably do the same if she would only ask, she couldn't put herself or anyone else on the line. She just didn't have that much courage.

The atmosphere in the saloon became too thick for her to breathe. She slipped out a side door, the smoky, dusty saloon air following in her wake, and looked around to get her bearings. She was in a small alley off the main road. The surrounding mountains kept the summer evenings cool and Meg closed her eyes, trying to block out the faint sounds of drunken men shouting to each other as they passed in the main street. A hand closed roughly around her mouth and dragged her back a few feet out of the weak pool of light that hung over the side entrance. Her eyes flew open and she struggled briefly before a menacing voice whispered, "Don't think about screaming. I could make things rough for you here in town."

Meg's strength seemed to ebb with those words. She went limp and her attacker took his hand away from her mouth, but forcibly kept her head turned away from him. It was all in vain because Meg already knew who her visitor was. Everyone who lived in town knew him well. He was an upstanding member of the community.

He continued to keep his voice low. "I want to know what Birch has told you."

She instinctively started to turn around, but his meaty hands stopped her. She said, "I don't know what you're talking about."

"You're cozy with Birch. Everyone in town who has eyes knows it. During all the time you've spent together, he must have told you what he thinks about his investigation." He was insistent. "Maybe he told you something when you two were dancing."

Meg's fright turned into impatience. "We barely talked while we were dancing. Besides, he's already got Felix Pierce. Why would he think there was someone else involved?"

"Don't underestimate Jefferson Birch."

I don't, Meg thought silently. She suddenly wished he were there. She hadn't packed her derringer tonight and even if she had, it would be hard to explain why she injured or killed this man. Aloud, she said, "We only talked about the fact that Felix Pierce was in jail. I congratulated him, he asked me if I thought he'd got the right man. I reminded him that Felix had been caught making a road withdrawal. What more proof could he want? That seemed to satisfy him."

There was silence for a minute. She almost thought her assailant had gone, but there was an audible sigh from behind her.

The voice spoke again. "I'll be glad when he leaves tomorrow."

She said in a tight voice, "We'll all be glad."

A hand gripped her elbow tightly, painfully. "If you run into him again tonight, just keep reassuring him that he has the right man." The pressure on her elbow was gone and so was her attacker.

Meg allowed herself to sag against the building wall briefly. Relief was replaced by rage. Her small white hands unconsciously clenched the silky fabric of her gown. She gulped in deep breaths of the night air in order to control her shaking limbs.

The side door opened, emitting light, smoke, and laughter along with a familiar figure. Meg automatically unclenched her hands, smoothed her skirt, and straightened up.

She asked, "Why did you come out this way? The main entrance is for customers."

Birch moved toward her. He smiled gently down at her. "I saw you leave a few minutes ago and when you didn't return, I became concerned and thought I'd come looking for you." He looked up and down the little side street. "It's pretty dark and secluded here. You should be more careful. Someone could take advantage of you."

He was very close to her. Meg was perfectly aware that her lips were within inches of his and she felt that small thrill that comes just before a kiss.

Meg couldn't take her eyes away from his. It felt right when he pulled her gently to him. Her arms went around his shoulders, pulling his face closer to her until their lips met.

She didn't know how long they were there, but when she pulled away, they were both breathing hard.

"I've been wanting to do that for a long time," said Birch. "You're a beautiful woman."

Meg blushed with pleasure. "Thank you." She reluctantly added, "I have to go back to my customers. Can we continue this up in my suite?"

*   *   *

He stayed all night. She found him to be a tender and passionate lover. In the morning, she woke up to find him dressed and ready to get his prisoner. Meg tried not to look too disappointed when he bent to kiss her good-bye, but he must have sensed her feelings.

"I'll be back," he said. "I think we have some unfinished business."

After he walked out the door, she threw on her robe and paced the room. Why had she allowed her attraction to this man to get out of hand? Meg realized that if Birch came back here, he'd be in real danger. Meg's pacing became agitated at the thought of Birch dying. Her face felt wet and when she reached up, Meg felt an unfamiliar moisture on her cheeks. She hadn't cried in years, since her husband David died, and she brushed angrily at her tears.

If Birch comes back here after escorting Felix Pierce to Jacksonville's jail, Meg thought, *I might have to tell him what I know. But not until then. I have to protect myself first.*

CHAPTER 21

THERE was a small crowd at the jailhouse. A wagon blocked the hitching post and an acting deputy was standing in front of the marshal's office door. Birch approached him and gave his name. The man nodded and let him through.

Stubbs was pacing the floor and rubbing the back of his neck. He looked up and shook his head when Birch came in. "I don't know how it happened."

Birch didn't know what Stubbs was talking about. "What happened?"

The marshal looked surprised. "The news has spread all around town. I'm surprised you didn't hear about it at breakfast."

"I haven't had breakfast yet," Birch said drily. He was getting impatient. "I thought I'd get here a little early and bring Pierce over to Meg's for breakfast before we head out."

A ghost of a smile appeared on Henry Stubbs's face. He rubbed his neck and shook his head again. "He won't be having breakfast anymore, son. Or supper. He hung himself this morning while I was gone to get breakfast."

Birch stared at Stubbs. "Hung himself? Why?"

"Well, I'd think that's obvious, don't you? He was remorseful about all the miners he'd robbed and killed."

"Pierce didn't strike me as the remorseful kind. Besides, we had a deal . . ." Birch trailed off, realizing that he'd said too much.

The marshal stopped and stared at him. "What kind of a deal?"

The ex–Texas Ranger silently cursed himself for slipping like that. He shrugged carelessly to cover up. "It doesn't matter anymore. He's dead and the deal's off."

"It matters to me, Birch. Start talking. What kind of a deal?" Stubbs leaned forward and asked, "What did he tell you?"

But Birch was not intimidated. He said evenly, "What Pierce told me was in confidence. It doesn't concern you."

The marshal backed off, moving to the other side of the room. He ran his hand through his hair. In a softer voice, he said, "Okay, Birch. But it might concern me. I've decided to investigate Pierce's death. I want to know why he killed himself. I happen to know that he has a wife and two daughters in Connecticut and was devoted to sending them money every month."

Birch cooled down. "For what it's worth, Marshal, he didn't tell me anything important. Nothing that could lead you to why he would hang himself. He didn't talk about jail like it was a humiliating experience. In fact, I have a feeling that he knew the inside of a jail cell pretty well. I didn't know about his family out East, though."

Stubbs took Birch in back to look over Pierce's cell. "I haven't touched anything yet."

Pierce's body had been cut down already, but everything seemed to be in place. The belt that Pierce hung from was still in place, fastened to a hook high on the wall opposite from the metal frame cot with the horsehair mattress. The body was laid out on the bed and the town doctor was bent over, examining it.

The doctor straightened up and addressed Stubbs. "Yep. He died from hanging, all right."

The body was carried out by two strong assistants, and the doctor followed. Stubbs and Birch were left alone. There was nothing more to derive from the cell, so they went back to the office.

"What about Pierce's wife, Marshal?"

Stubbs looked uncomfortable as he thought about the unpleasant task facing him. "I guess I'll have to notify her and put the saloon up for sale. Unless she wants to come out here and run it herself."

"Well," Birch said, "I'd better head for Jacksonville. I have to report to the sheriff."

Stubbs stuck his hand out and they shook. "Good luck, son. And good-bye."

Birch paused at the door and said, "I may be back."

Before he left town, Birch went back to the Rogue River Saloon to see Meg one more time. Maybe she could help him make sense of Pierce's suicide. Something was bothering him, but he couldn't quite put his finger on it.

He ordered breakfast and gave the serving girl a message for Meg. Within a few minutes, Meg appeared, wearing a light gray morning dress and a sparkle in her eyes.

"Hello stranger," she said lightly. "I thought you'd be gone by now."

Birch smiled slightly and shook his head. "I guess you haven't heard. Pierce hung himself in his cell this morning."

Meg's face lost its color. For a moment, she looked frightened, but tried to cover up her violent reaction.

In a shaky voice, she replied, "I'm sorry to hear that about a fellow saloon owner."

Birch leaned forward and took her hand. He felt her try to resist, but he held onto it firmly. "I don't know what's going on around here, Meg, but maybe you'd better let me in on it. That was no accident, was it? Pierce was murdered."

Meg grew silent. In a composed voice, she replied, "I wouldn't know anything about it. Does it look like murder?"

He felt frustrated. Every time Meg started to get close to him, something would happen to make her pull away. It was as if she didn't trust him. Or didn't trust herself. One thing he was certain of, Meg was frightened of someone or something.

He shook his head. "No, of course not. It's just a gut feeling."

"Well, you can't always rely on gut feelings, Jefferson," Meg said heatedly. "Pierce is dead. Can't you just accept that? Maybe this will put an end to the road withdrawals."

She stood up abruptly. "I have work to do. Go to Jacksonville and make your report."

With that, she turned away and left.

When Birch's breakfast arrived, he ate in thoughtful silence.

CHAPTER 22

ON the road to Jacksonville, Birch was deep in thought. Was Felix Pierce the one and only leader of the outlaw gang? Why had he hung himself in the cell?

Birch just couldn't accept that Pierce would commit suicide because he felt remorse for robbing and killing all of those miners. Pierce may have felt fear, but he hadn't expressed regret for what he'd done. And he had emphatically denied having killed those miners.

As a Texas Ranger, Birch had known many killers and they all had one thing in common: their eyes were as flat and cold as a rattlesnake's just before striking its prey. Felix Pierce didn't have the eyes of a killer, he had the eyes of a gambler.

Something was bothering Birch about the jail cell. The belt on the hook, the bed against the opposite wall, but nothing had been moved, according to the marshal. Then it hit him: nothing had been moved, yet Pierce had managed to hang himself without moving the cot over to climb up on and kick away. Wasn't that how most suicides would do it?

So who could have murdered Felix Pierce? It had to be someone in town, someone who was respected, even feared. It had to be a man who was known to the whole community, and whose activities were probably known to the whole community.

Birch recalled Meg's reaction when she was told about Pierce's death. He remembered the look on Pierce's face

159

when he was told that he would be spending a night in the Grant's Pass jail cell. Pierce had begged Birch to take him to Jacksonville that same afternoon after he had agreed to reveal names and places.

Pierce's last words before entering Grant's Pass, "Please don't say anything to anyone concerning my previous offer to you. It still stands if you get me safely to Jacksonville tomorrow."

If.

Birch's mind reviewed everything again. He'd almost forgotten about the yellow bandannas tied to the Ridley brothers' saddles. What were they for? The kerchiefs must signal to the outlaw band that the Ridleys were miners traveling to Jacksonville with gold. It seemed to be about the only thing those kerchiefs could denote.

Birch shook his head. It all seemed too complicated. All the clues seemed to go in about three different directions. Maybe that was the key, he thought. Maybe there was more than one man in town who was involved in the road withdrawals. And Birch suspected one man in particular.

But first, he needed some information and the only way to make sure the information was right was to continue on to Jacksonville.

CHAPTER 23

SHERIFF Brent Calhoun was sitting at his desk when Birch arrived. He stood up and shook hands with the tall, lean ex-Ranger. "I hear you've been stirring things up back in Grant's Pass, Birch." There was an amused glint in his eye as he said it.

Birch pushed his hat back off his forehead. "Well, Sheriff, I don't know if I was the one who started things, but Marshal Stubbs is out one deputy, and this morning Felix Pierce, the prisoner I was supposed to bring here, hung himself in his cell."

Calhoun sat down at his desk and stared down at it for a moment. The only sound that could be heard was the tap-tapping of the pencil he held in his hand. Then he looked up. "Well, now. Don't that beat all. I guess that means you're finished with this case, Birch."

"Not quite yet, Sheriff."

Calhoun smiled. "You trying to cost this county more money?"

Birch was serious. He said, "No, Sheriff, I'm trying to save the county some money. I need information and I probably won't get a straight answer in Grant's Pass, so I came to you."

"I'll do my best, Birch." Calhoun looked up at Birch with admiration. "Boy, when you get hold of a case, you won't let it go, will you?"

"But it's not finished yet. I can't walk away from it now."

The sheriff shook his head and said, "Most men would consider it closed because the leader of the gang is dead, Birch. The gang will break up and scatter without the leader. Eventually, the rest of the outlaws will be caught and jailed."

Birch smiled. "There's more than one leader in this case. I have reason to believe that there were two, both living in Grant's Pass, leading respectable lives." He turned the conversation back to his original request. "Now I need to know if there were any yellow- or saffron-colored bandannas found on the dead miners. And what about the miners who are still alive? Did they mention having been given a bandanna prior to their trip to Jacksonville?"

Birch kept the sheriff busy all afternoon searching through both old and new *wanted* posters. He wanted every lead followed up.

By suppertime, he'd found out several useful pieces of information that tied another suspect to the road withdrawals.

". . . so you're saying that he arrived in Grant's Pass just about a month before Felix Pierce showed up?"

Calhoun nodded and pointed emphatically at the yellowed *wanted* poster. "And neither man has a record shown under their current names. Pierce's real name must be Jack Cronin. Cronin has a wife and children in Connecticut. Two girls."

"And Cronin's wanted in Massachusetts for assaulting a man in a poker game and running off with the money," Birch mused. "I'm surprised that he didn't break off contact with his wife and kids. He must have had strong ties there."

"I don't know about that, but he did have this partner, Frank Stanley. Look at this picture." Calhoun indicated the pen-and-ink drawing of Stanley. "What I can't believe is that I didn't check out the other man more thoroughly. He's more dangerous, yet he's been running Grant's Pass for almost six months."

Birch nodded. "I know of him. Committed several robberies in the Southwest Territory—Oklahoma and Texas mostly—and murdered ten people in what is now known as the Mill Creek Massacre. The Rangers were actually called up to Mill Creek in Oklahoma when that happened. Stanley's a cold-blooded killer."

The sheriff sat back in his chair and stretched. "I'll bet that Cronin was riding with him in Oklahoma."

Birch abruptly stood up. "Thank you for the information, Sheriff. I'd better get supper and some shut-eye if I'm going back to Grant's Pass tomorrow."

Calhoun stood up as well. "You're not going back up there alone, Birch. I'll send some of my best men with you. Stanley's a killer."

Birch's face was impassive. "You hired me to do a job and I aim to do it. Save your men for hunting down the rest of the gang members."

Calhoun persisted. "I hired you to get information for me, not to get yourself killed. If you won't let me send any of my men, take me along."

"No. But thanks for the offer."

Calhoun pounded his fist on his desk in frustration. "Damn it, Birch. I don't approve of heroics. Let me do something."

Birch smiled slightly and said, "I'm hungry. You can buy me supper."

CHAPTER 24

BIRCH waited until late afternoon of the following day to start out for Grant's Pass. He could probably catch Luke Stone at Meg's before the reverend was in his cups, yet he didn't want to attract attention. He would get there Saturday night when everyone would be out at the saloons and in the street.

Saturday night was as rowdy as when he'd first ridden into town the week before. Loud whoops and the sound of fist meeting flesh came from Stinky's as he rode by. He was tempted to stop in and look for Swede, but he had more important things to do at the moment. When he got inside the Rogue River Saloon & Gambling Parlor, he looked around for Meg O'Malley, but she was nowhere in sight. When he stepped up to the bar, Shorty recognized him and raised his eyebrows. Birch signaled for a beer.

"You want me to get one of the girls to find Meg for you?" Shorty asked as he placed a beer in front of Birch.

He waved away Birch's silver dollar. Apparently everyone knew that Birch was Meg's lover now. He wasn't used to this familiarity, but didn't want to make a scene. He put his coin away and said, "Not right now. I need to find Luke Stone. Do you know him by sight?"

Shorty grunted. "Yeah. He used to come in here on Sundays to preach, but Meg wasn't crazy about the saloon turning into a church on Sundays—especially when Stone got a little too free with our liquor supply."

Shorty laughed at the thought. "He used to stand up every fifteen minutes and say, 'Bartender, God would like to buy another round.' Unfortunately, God wasn't real good at paying, so it got to be too expensive. Lucky for Stone that Pierce offered to open the Red Palace as a House of God on Sundays."

Yeah, lucky for Pierce, too, Birch thought silently. With Stone coming in regularly and plying the worshippers with drink, someone would open up about their motherlode or the fact that next week they'd be going to Jacksonville with a haul. And Stone probably never had a clue as to why Pierce really offered the Red Palace as a place of worship . . . or did he?

"Anyway," Shorty continued, "I haven't seen him yet tonight. He usually comes in later." He took out his rag and slowly wiped down the bar while pointedly ignoring customers clamoring for another shot of Red Eye. They could wait. "You might even catch him on the trail, if you decide to head up toward the mining camp."

Birch drained his beer and set the empty mug down on the bar. "Thanks, Shorty. I'll be back."

He got back on Cactus and rode out of town without meeting anyone he knew. About fifteen minutes outside of town, he met Stone and Dewey.

Dewey was the first to recognize and greet Birch. "Good evening, Jefferson. I heard you brought Felix Pierce in."

Luke Stone looked more surprised than Dewey to see Birch. "By golly. It's good to see you, Birch. What brings you back to these parts? Not the gold fever, I hope."

Birch smiled and shook his head. "I'm afraid not."

"Probably just as well. Only claim open along this part of the river now is Jake and Carl Ridley's old one." Stone frowned. "You wouldn't want that one. I heard that Carl salted it so some fool will come along and snap it up without thinking twice."

Birch interrupted Stone's rambling. "Actually, I came back to ask you a couple more questions. Between you and Dewey, I hope I can get some answers. Who besides the Ridleys was given a yellow bandanna or some other brightly colored kerchief?"

The miners looked at each other for a moment. Dewey finally said, "Elijah Stearns was found with one tied around his hatband. Come to think of it, I have seen some of the other boys around camp with gold-colored bandannas. I don't know about the others. I think we'd have to ask."

Stone added, "And they were all robbed on the way to Jacksonville. Pierce gave the Ridleys their bandannas, but we don't know if he gave one to Elijah Stearns."

"Wait a minute," Dewey said slowly. "I don't know if this means anything, but the morning Lije started for Jacksonville, I walked by the marshal's office and picked up that yellow bandanna. Lije had stopped to talk to Marshal Stubbs, and dropped it. I don't know if the marshal gave it to him or not, but I've never seen such a fuss made over a bandanna before."

Birch asked, "What do you mean, a fuss?"

"Well, I'd just come out of the dry goods store and spotted something yellow lying in the middle of the street in front of the marshal's office," Dewey answered. "I picked it up and asked Marshal Stubbs about it. Marshal Stubbs told me it was Lije's lucky charm. I'd seen Lije riding out of town at a good pace, but the marshal insisted that he run after Lije to return the bandanna." Dewey shook his head, then looked up at Birch. "Could it be?"

"Guess I'll find out soon enough." Birch wheeled Cactus around. "Let's go have a drink."

Meg was waiting outside her saloon when Birch and his two companions got there.

There was fear in her eyes as well as pleasure. She said, "I didn't expect you back so soon."

Birch dismounted Cactus. "I still have unfinished business here."

"Jefferson, I . . ."

He gave her a sharp look.

She tried again. "Will you be staying with me?"

"I don't know." He escorted her into the saloon. Stone and Dewey had already joined the revelry. Birch ordered a whiskey.

A few minutes later, Meg came back up to him. "I think we need to talk." She motioned him outside.

Meg walked to the end of the wooden sidewalk and turned around to face Birch. "You found out the truth."

Birch had casually leaned up against a post. "You knew all the time."

She walked quickly up to him, beseeching. "Don't you see? I couldn't say anything. He'd kill me. Everyone in town knew."

Birch laughed, a short bark. "So you let all those miners be robbed of their hard-earned gold and even let a few of them get killed."

"It would have happened anyway," Meg said angrily. "I couldn't have done anything to help."

"You went to Jacksonville several times. You could have told the sheriff. But as long as some of the gold was spent in your saloon and all the other businesses, none of you would lift a finger."

"Pierce and Stubbs had eyes and ears everywhere. How was I to know that the sheriff in Jacksonville wasn't one of them?" Meg moved closer to Birch. "Jefferson, you've got to believe me. I was afraid to say anything."

He gave her a stony look. It was clear that he was unmoved. "And when I came along? Why didn't you say anything then? I can understand being slightly cautious, but what about the other night? Couldn't you even trust me after the other night? No, Meg. By keeping quiet, you're as guilty as they are."

Out of the darkness, a voice asked, "As guilty as who?"

Birch turned. He knew that voice. He called out. "As guilty as you are, Marshal."

Stubbs stepped into the light, his gun pointed at Birch. "Why don't you and me take a little ride?"

Meg had shrunk back against the building as if she wanted to be invisible.

Stubbs noticed her.

"You too, Meg."

CHAPTER 25

STUBBS had taken Birch's guns. Meg rode behind Birch on Cactus. They rode slowly so Stubbs could keep an eye on them.

Birch felt Meg's arms around his waist and her body pressing up against his back. It reminded him of the times Audrey would ride behind him when they were first married.

Birch had thought that Meg could help him forget his late wife, but Meg wasn't like Audrey. If Audrey had been in Meg's position, she would have done the right thing. She would have told Birch about Stubbs and Pierce. Meg's first thought was self-preservation. Birch couldn't blame her, but he wasn't sure he would ever be able to trust her or love her as he had Audrey.

Of course, none of that would matter if they didn't live to see tomorrow.

Stubbs's gun remained pointed at them until an opportunity was presented for Birch to disarm him. The opportunity came in the form of a group of drunken revellers. Birch, seeing the chance earlier, had slowed his horse down slightly. The marshal lowered his gun as they passed in order to make their presence less conspicuous, even to a bunch of rowdys.

Birch lunged toward the gun. He couldn't leap off Cactus because Meg was directly behind him, but he got Stubbs off balance for a moment. Birch took advantage of this to swing Meg down to the ground.

171

"Run back to the saloon!" He ordered her. "Get help."

Stubbs fired at Meg and hit a barrel of grain that was parked by the general store's door. *Thunk!* went the bullet and grain spilled onto the wooden walkway, making a hissing sound as it escaped.

Meg stumbled on her skirts, but with Cactus acting as a shield, she made it to the shelter of the general store and disappeared into the shadows. Stubbs fired a few more shots in her direction while Birch spurred Cactus into action.

Stubbs followed. They were headed out of town. Birch wasn't sure what he was going to do without a gun. *I guess I'll have to make it up as I go along,* he thought wryly, *just like last time.*

He was a good quarter of a mile away from town and a few hundred yards ahead of his pursuer when he saw his chance. Birch slowed down and reached into his saddlebag for the rope he'd used the other day. He deftly looped one rope end around a limb, then tied it around a limb on the other side of the road. He leapt off Cactus, slapped his horse's quarters, and took up a hidden position near his trap.

The thrumming of horse's hooves striking the beaten dirt road grew closer. The marshal had his gun out and was taking aim at Cactus when the horse kept going and Stubbs was stopped in midair.

Birch heard a satisfying thud as Stubbs landed hard on his back. Birch followed the groan and found Henry Stubbs lying a few feet behind the rope.

The horses hesitated and stopped about fifty yards down. Stubbs's gun was nowhere to be seen. He must have dropped it when the rope got him.

"Sumbitch," Stubbs moaned. "Sumbitch. I'm gonna kill you."

Birch was reaching up to take down the rope to tie Stubbs up. He looked around and found that Henry Stubbs had gotten up and was coming at him. Birch was tackled just as the first end of the rope was loosened. It fell to the middle of the road.

He fell hard against a tree, scraping his shoulder. He pulled himself up and rushed the marshal, getting a left jab in to Stubbs's gut. Stubbs let out an "Oof!" and staggered back. Birch moved in again, expecting to finish Stubbs off with a few more punches, but the marshal had a constitution like a bulldog. He sent a haymaker to Birch's jaw that stunned him and forced them both back onto the road.

Stubbs is a powerful son of a bitch, Birch thought. Before Birch could clear his head, Stubbs was tightening the rope around his neck with all his might. Birch clawed at it, desperate for air, but Stubbs seemed to sense his weakening will and gave the rope an extra twist.

Birch couldn't focus. Words floated above him. He knew Stubbs was speaking to him because they were the only two around. And Birch wouldn't be around for long.

"You thought you had it all figured out. I'm the leader. We call ourselves the Bankers. Get it? We made withdrawals on this road like it was a bank."

Stubbs's chuckle sounded faint as Birch began to lose consciousness.

His fingertips brushed against a cold, hard metal object—Stubbs's gun! He willed himself to stay conscious just long enough for his fingers to close around the gun handle.

A moment later, there was a loud gunshot. Stubbs's grip on the rope slackened. Birch held the smoking gun. He tore the rope off and gasped for air.

A bloody rose bloomed on Stubbs's chest.

Birch stood up and took a deep breath, then went after the horses.

CHAPTER 26

BEFORE Birch slung the body over the horse, he took Henry Stubbs's badge off and placed it in his shirt pocket, next to the badge identifying him as a Tisdale detective. The badges clanked together like two silver dollars. He only took a few minutes to reach Grant's Pass.

Men and women were loitering around outside of the saloons as Birch rode into town. Swede, Stone, and Dewey were just getting ready to mount up. Swede spotted Birch first.

He called out, "We were just getting ready to come after you."

Stone and Dewey had already abandoned their horses and were running up to the inert body slung over the saddle. Birch reached up and touched the rope burn around his neck. Meg had joined the crowd. She looked up at him, but when he looked back, she turned her head away in shame.

Wolfgang had joined them.

Birch dismounted and handed the dead marshal's reins over to Dewey. "Will you take care of it? I don't think he's alive, but I'm not a doctor."

Birch reached into his pocket and brought out the marshal's badge. He walked over to Swede and gave it to him.

"You're acting marshal until I get to Jacksonville tomorrow and inform Sheriff Calhoun about all of this."

"But Birch," Swede protested, "I know nothing about being a marshal."

"If that's the case," Birch replied, "you'll probably do a better job than he did." He indicated the body. Then he turned and led his horse toward the Gold Hills Hotel.

Meg fell in step with him. They were silent for part of the way. Then she put her hand on his arm.

He stopped, still not looking at her.

"Jefferson, please. Don't go. Let's start over."

"I can't, Meg." His voice came out toneless, lifeless. "I don't think I trust you."

Her voice was tight, desperate. Birch could almost hear the tears in her voice. "You could take Stubbs's job. You could clean up this town. You could trust me. I care about you."

Birch shook his head and started walking again. "It wouldn't work, Meg. I'd always be looking over my shoulder."

The next morning, Birch packed his saddlebags, settled up his hotel bill, and rode out of town. As he reached the outskirts of Grant's Pass, he gave in to temptation and turned for one last look. The street was nearly empty and quiet after last night's excitement. It almost looked serene except for the figure of a woman standing just inside the door of the Rogue River Saloon & Gambling Parlor. She seemed to be facing in Birch's direction. He wondered if it was Meg.

Birch had stayed in some dirty towns when he was working as a Ranger and he'd seen his share of thieves, liars, and murderers, but he'd never felt bad about shooting them or putting them behind bars. So why, he asked himself, did he regret leaving this town?

He knew the answer without thinking about it for too long: it was too bad about Meg.

shooting them or putting them behind bars. So why, he asked himself, did he regret leaving this town?

He knew the answer without thinking about it for too long: it was too bad about Meg.

If you have enjoyed this book and would like to receive details of other Walker Western titles, please write to:

Western Editor
Walker and Company
720 Fifth Avenue
New York, NY 10019